MW00874044

Not an Heiress

Not an Heiress

A Sequel to Discovering Mr. Darcy

LEENIE BROWN

LEENIE B BOOKS
HALIFAX

Contents

Dear Reader,

This novella is part of my *Dash of Darcy and Companions Collection*. These *Pride and Prejudice* inspired stories are quick, sweet reads designed to fit perfectly into a busy life.

Dash of Darcy titles in this collection will focus on Darcy and Elizabeth, while each *Companion Story* will focus on characters from *Pride and Prejudice* other than Darcy and Elizabeth and will be a sequel to a *Dash of Darcy* story.

The books in this collection are numbered in the order in which they were published and contain a complete HEA (happily ever after) for the hero and heroine. However, you may wish to know that all *Companion Stories* will reference events in the *Dash of Darcy* story to which they are a sequel, so reading those stories together will provide the greatest enjoyment.

Thank you for selecting to spend time with this

story. It is my desire that you will find a sweet escape within its pages.

Happy Reading!

Leenie B.

Prologue

Mr. Bennet settled back in his chair and studied the lady who sat in front of his desk. It was not their first meeting. They had spent several hours in various conversations during his latest stay at Pemberley.

"You are still of the belief that Colonel Fitzwilliam holds a tendre for my Mary?"

Lady Catherine de Bourgh liked Mr. Bennet. He did not dance around a subject — one could be direct with the man. He was also not the sort of gentleman to dismiss a lady simply because she wore a dress and was capable of bearing children. "I am certain. My brother, Lord Matlock, informs me that his son Richard has spent the best part of the season attempting to find a wife."

"That does not signify that he holds my Mary in regard."

Lady Catherine smiled. "Perhaps, but I find it curious that each lady has been found lacking despite her beauty and fortune."

Mr. Bennet shrugged. "He has simply not found that for which he is looking. It is not so unusual."

"Mr. Bennet, I must disagree. He has found the one he needs to marry. He is just unwilling to accept her because she does not yet have a fortune." She saw Mr. Bennet's head begin to shake, but she was not about to allow him to contradict her. She had adequate proof that her supposition was correct, so she shared a sampling. "His father heard him asking one very well dowered young lady whether she read Fordyce, and when she replied in the negative, he thanked her for the dance and departed. He never approached her again."

Mr. Bennet's eyes had grown wide, and he had leaned forward eagerly interested.

"My nephew has also grumbled loudly that most of the ladies he has taken for a picnic or a drive do not consider it their place to care for the children. They would prefer a nurse or governess see to the task of raising the next generation of offspring, which you know is not unusual, but it is the opposite of how your daughter views the responsibilities of a mother."

Mr. Bennet nodded. Mary had always spoken firmly in defense of a mother's role in caring for her children. And that defense often contained a quote from the scriptures such as that bit about Timothy's mother. Mr. Bennet scratched just below his ear. He should be able to remember it as oft as he had heard it.

"Those ladies also were never approached again." Lady Catherine straightened the hem of her sleeve. "Mark my words, Mr. Bennet, my nephew was comparing them to Miss Mary and has found them wanting."

It was logic that Mr. Bennet could not deny. "So, you have devised a way to make my Mary acceptable to him?"

Lady Catherine inclined her head and gave a half shrug. "I should like him to accept her regardless of what those documents say." She pointed to the packet of papers lying before Mr. Bennet. Then with a last fidget of straightening her sleeve, she held his gaze. "However, I intend to force the issue much as I did with Darcy."

A sparkle of amusement shone in Mr. Bennet's

eyes. She had hoped his wish to be amused by the folly of others might assist her in her scheme, and it appeared it would.

"I am not opposed to a compromise," he said, "as long as it is evident that both will be happy with the results."

"I could not agree more. I should not wish either unhappy, for I shall, after all, be forced to live with that happiness or lack thereof."

Mr. Bennet nodded slowly. "Then I give my permission to arrange the match however you see fit." He touched the place where he had signed the documents to ensure the ink had dried before he folded them and pushed them across the desk toward Lady Catherine. "The second son of an earl is not a bad catch for my Mary."

Lady Catherine allowed it to be so as she picked up the papers from the desk and placed them in the bag she had brought with her. "I should very much like to have you and your family visit Rosings in one month from today."

Mr. Bennet's brows furrowed.

Lady Catherine rose. "Your wife will not be opposed to a wedding breakfast in Kent, will she?" It was such fun to see a man's eyes pop open wide and his mouth drop open. She had enjoyed creating that expression when just a girl, and it seemed the pleasure did not fade as one aged. She waited while Mary's father mentally gathered himself.

"I should think she will be delighted," Mr. Bennet finally managed to reply.

"The earl and countess will also be in attendance." Her lips pursed as she struggled to keep a grin in check. "I would advise you to bring whatever documents are needed for all to be settled quickly. I shall see that a license is secured." She extended her hand to Mr. Bennet. "I do so like doing business with a man who knows how to come to the point quickly."

Mr. Bennet gave her hand a firm shake to seal their deal. "You will ensure she is happy?" he asked, still holding Lady Catherine's hand.

She nodded. Lady Catherine could understand his hesitance. Parents of any true worth always worried for the happiness of their children. "I would not accept any less than pure delight." She smiled as he lifted her hand and kissed it. "I shall see you in one month?"

"One month," he assured her.

She moved to exit the room but then stopped

just short of the door. "You will not mention the need for the visit, will you? I should hate for the surprise to be ruined for Miss Mary." Indeed, her plans would likely come to naught if word reached Mary before they could be put into action.

"Not a word until three weeks hence." He chuckled. "I can only endure the raptures of my wife in minuscule amounts, and the mere thought of being invited to an estate such as Rosings and being in the presence of a real lady will send her soaring."

Lady Catherine chuckled as she reached for the door handle. She had witnessed some of Mrs. Bennet's raptures over the past three years, and she did not envy Mr. Bennet's place in having to endure them as often as she suspected he did. "You are a wise man, Mr. Bennet." She pulled the door open. "One month," she repeated and waited to get a nod of acceptance before exiting his study.

Chapter 1

Mary Bennet tucked the book she had just finished reading back on the shelf and pulled out another. The selection of books at Rosings was not small, but — she sighed, there were just not enough books of substance, at least, not the substance she sought. She flipped through the pages covered in verse.

There was only so much poetry she could read, and she was certain she had surpassed her limit. In her opinion, poetry did nothing to secure the mind in the realities of propriety. In fact, lately, it had done the exact opposite. It had her dreaming of walks in the forest and along streams with her hand in that of a very handsome gentleman — a gentleman who was not within her reach.

She shoved the book back onto the shelf. Poetry was not what she needed. He would be here soon.

She needed to have something more serious to read. Something that would keep her mind from wandering to his wide shoulders and muscular calves. Young ladies should not have such thoughts, especially young ladies who were determined to be an example of propriety to one and all. However, no matter how she tried, Colonel Richard Fitzwilliam could not be thought of as serenely as other men. It was really quite vexing how he tormented her with thoughts that caused her to smile at impropriety. A sermon was needed and the sooner, the better.

"If Lady Catherine is looking for me, I will be at the parsonage," Mary told Fletcher, Rosings' butler, as she tied on her bonnet in preparation for her walk. "I will not be long."

"The parsonage?" Lady Catherine de Bourgh stood in the doorway to her sitting room just down the hall from where Mary was attempting her escape. "We have guests arriving. It would not do for you to be gone when they arrive, and if I know my nephews, they will be early just to vex me."

"I will not be long," Mary tried to keep the pleading tone from her voice. "I only wish to borrow a book from my cousin."

Lady Catherine's eyebrows rose. "Are there not enough books in the library?" She knew precisely the sort of book Mary sought, but it was better to not let the young lady know.

"It is lacking in sermons." Mary looked at Lady Catherine's toes. Lady Catherine was not pleased to have her library or any part of her home criticized, nor was she particularly fond of Mary's choice of reading material. Mary had endured more than one lecture on broadening her repertoire.

"It is lacking in nothing that a young woman should need." Lady Catherine had taken a liking to Mary when she met the young lady at Pemberley the second summer after Lady Catherine's nephew Fitzwilliam Darcy and Mary's sister Elizabeth had married.

Mary was the most likely of the three youngest Bennet sisters, who were in residence that summer, to need improvement and need it the earliest. Lydia and Kitty did not seem to lack an interest in society the way Mary did, nor were Lydia or Kitty in as great a need of a husband since they were younger than Mary.

However, there was something else that

endeared the young lady to Lady Catherine — nothing that could be quantified beyond a spirit of gentleness mingled with a will of iron. She smiled. It would be lovely to have such a lady added to her collection of relatives in a closer fashion. It had not escaped her notice how often she found the young lady watching Richard nor how often Richard found reason to be in the presence of Mary.

Mary's shoulders drooped. "I have faithfully read the novels you gave me and the book of poems. May I not read just one book of sermons?"

Lady Catherine pursed her lips. "One book?"

Mary nodded.

Lady Catherine sighed. "Very well, but be quick."

Mary dipped a curtsey. "I will, my lady."

Lady Catherine watched her scurry out the door. It might be best if Mary were gone when the others arrived. It would make discussing her with Darcy and Elizabeth a good deal easier.

"Have the tea things brought in half an hour," she said to Fletcher before returning to her sitting room. She sighed. The house was so empty these days without Anne and Mrs. Jenkinson to keep her company. It was partially why she had requested of Mr. Bennet that Mary come to stay with her.

She chuckled. Her meeting with the gentleman had been very productive. Not only had she gotten permission for Mary to come stay at Rosings, but she had also received his blessing to play at match-making for the one whom she considered his least-likely-to-marry daughter.

She settled into a chair that stood in just the right place to see the drive and took up her stitch-ing. She would not be caught unawares. Her nephews might attempt to ruffle her feathers by thwarting her carefully scheduled life, but they would not succeed. The thought of ruining their fun with a bit of her own pleased her excessively. She would know when her guests had arrived well before they had stepped one foot from their car-riage.

She did not have to wait very long. The tea ser-vice was just being laid out when she spotted them. Darcy's fine carriage appeared first, and then Richard followed, seated high on his horse.

He was a fine specimen of a gentleman. Even she could see that. For all the detractors that found him less handsome than his cousin — which he was since there were few as handsome as Darcy — there were an equal number who found him enticing, especially when he was riding his horse or causing a general stir with some fascinating tale. Mary would be a very fortunate young lady to have such a husband.

And he would do well to have a sensible and devoted wife. Lady Catherine gave a little shrug. It was perhaps Richard who was getting the better end of the bargain. Mary was no wallflower, no matter how much she might attempt to be one. True, she did not shine like Jane or sparkle like Elizabeth, but she was not without charm. It was just that hers was the kind of beauty that lay quietly, waiting to be noticed.

Lady Catherine laid aside her stitching and watched as the carriage came to a stop and Richard jumped down to claim Alexander from his parents. He would make an excellent father despite his tendencies to exuberance and impropriety. She could not help smiling as he trotted off toward the garden with a laughing child on his shoulder.

It appeared the moment had come, and she smoothed her skirts nervously as she rose to greet Darcy and Elizabeth. With neither of the objects of her scheming present, now would be the best time to inform her other guests of her intentions to see Mary and Richard happily wed.

~*~*~

Mary did not spend very long at the parsonage, just a few minutes with Charlotte, hearing about the antics and accomplishments of the two young Collins boys and inquiring after Charlotte's health as she was preparing for the arrival of a third child. Then, after a mere five minutes of listening to Mr. Collins wax eloquent on the book he was lending, she was free to leave.

Charlotte was so very good at distracting her husband when he began meandering. Mary hoped that when she married, she might find a sensible husband. A parson would be nice — one with a good living or two. Such an arrangement would afford her the comfort she desired. Of course, the wedding papers would have to be created in such a fashion as to leave her and any children she might have with ample means to live without relying on the charity of relations too much if she should be left a widow. She did not wish to have to worry about such things as her mother did.

She sighed. If only she were an heiress. Then,

she would have a home and a husband that would provide everything for which she wished, but she was not an heiress, and so she must put fanciful and imprudent dreams out of her head. Colonel Fitzwilliam would not be hers, no matter what her heart's desire was on the matter.

She rambled along the tree lined lane with her book under her arm and mind firmly engaged with one of those imprudent dreams. In this one, she was walking this very lane leaning on the colonel's arm. She sighed. She had noticed how his arms had been so very firm and strong whenever she had had the chance to walk with him at Pemberley. So strong. She wondered if a parson would be as well muscled as a colonel. She supposed not. After all, a colonel spent his time in riding and other gen-tlemanly pursuits while a parson spent his time studying. Reading, though a magnificent exercise for the brain, did very little to strengthen the body.

It was on these things that she was pondering when she turned from the lane and entered Ros-ing's garden in the exact place where Richard was being chased by a squealing Alexander. She was not prepared to confront him just now. She had not had a moment to read anything grave! How was she to not allow her mind to be filled with him when she had fed it with nothing but poetry and novels? So, being totally unprepared, she was doomed to be struck most soundly by his presence and the charming prospect of him as he might be as a father. Had Alexander not stopped when she appeared at the edge of the garden, she might have been able to slip back into the lane and find a less provocative route to the house or a place to sit and read a bit before she ventured back into the garden.

"Miss Mary!" Colonel Fitzwilliam drew to a halt not far from her. "I did not expect to see you at Rosings? Are you visiting your cousin?" He directed the question to her but turned to make certain Alexander was still close. The child had moved, but not away. He had taken a few steps toward Mary and was tipping his head to the side as if he were trying to figure out who she was. "It is Aunt Mary," Richard told him. "Mama's sister." He held out his arms in invitation to Alexander. "Come. Give your greetings as a proper young gentleman should."

It did not take more than a minute for the child to find his way into Richard's arms where he managed to give Mary a sweetly proper greeting by repeating everything that Richard told him to say.

"It is good to see you, Alexander," Mary replied. "Is your mama in the house?"

Alexander twisted to look back at the house. He pointed and babbled about mama and biscuits.

"Ah, yes, Uncle Richard did promise you a biscuit, did he not?" said Richard. "Shall we invite Aunt Mary to join us and share our biscuits?"

Alexander's brows furrowed.

"She will not eat many," Richard assured him. "Shall we ask her?"

A smile crept across the young boy's face, and he nodded his agreement.

"Very well. Miss Mary, will you join us for biscuits?"

"And tea?" Mary asked Alexander.

"Tea." His head bobbed up and down.

Richard, extending an arm to Mary, steeled himself for the pleasant jolt he always felt when she accepted his assistance. He had not prepared in vain, for as she lay her hand on his arm, there it was again. If only he could find a woman of the ton with a substantial dowry who could cause the same reaction in him. He had searched diligently for three months now, attending soiree after soiree and dancing with every quiet, soulful-eyed debutante he could find. When none had been able to attract him as Mary did, he had cast the net so far as to dance with the more exuberant and popular young ladies. Still, with not success.

"How long are you visiting your cousin?" He hoped it would not be long. For if it was, he would have to go back to London and its balls and parties before he could be reminded too fully of all that Mary was. A fresh memory of her would do nothing to assist him in his attempt not to compare every young lady to her.

"I am not visiting my cousin," she said.

"You are not?"

"No, Lady Catherine has asked me to come stay with her. She misses Anne."

Oh, this was not good. Not good at all. He would have to create an escape plan. Perhaps a supposed letter from a friend could call him away. "Are you staying long?"

"Indefinitely," Mary replied. "Or until I find a husband. Your aunt is insistent that she can see me well-matched before the end of next season." Unfortunately, it would not be to the man she desired, but one did not always get what one wished.

Richard had known she would eventually marry. She must. It was not as if she had the independent means to live on her own, and he supposed she did not wish to spend her whole life without a husband and family. When Alexander was just an infant, Mary had visited Pemberley and had been so naturally good at calming the child and tending to his needs. She was born to be a mother. It really was too bad she was not an heiress, for he would very much like for her to be the mother of his children.

"Next season? So a year or nearly so?"

Mary shrugged. "Unless a worthy candidate stumbles into Kent and presents himself before then. I will be given some time to visit my family, but the majority of my life shall be here — under Lady Catherine's tutelage."

"I am surprised Darcy has not mentioned this." It was unlike his cousin to keep information from him.

"I only arrived three weeks ago. Lady Catherine thought it unnecessary to inform him since he would be arriving for his annual visit in such a short time."

Alexander began to squirm as they got closer to the house and demanded that he be allowed to walk.

"Will you hold my hand?" Mary asked him.

He agreed with alacrity, and Richard was forced to relinquish both his possession of the child and Mary's hand. It was just as well, he supposed, as he walked beside them. It was not as if he had a hope of ever truly claiming her hand, so he had best get used to seeing it claimed by another.

This thought did nothing to ease his displeasure, nor did the knowledge that the gentleman stealing her hand away from him was only two years old and her nephew. He shook himself. A letter. He must write a letter to himself and then ride out and have it posted, for an escape was definitely necessary.

Chapter 2

Tea was tolerably good. Not that the leaves were less than excellent, nor were they improperly steeped. The tea tray held a variety of delicacies all prepared to perfection. It was not even so much the company that tainted the tea.

Mary enjoyed seeing her sister and Darcy, and Alexander was ready to entertain with his pacing back and forth between the adults, looking very much like a little gentleman with his hands clasped behind his back. He would come to a stop before one of them and would then tip his head and wait patiently for the person in front of whom he stood to notice him before he would ask for a cake or biscuit, always adding a "peez" to the end of the request. His little brows would furrow, and his lips would purse in displeasure if he was denied, but instead of protesting, he would simply find another person to petition. Eventually, his mother decided it was time for him to go to the nursery. With a great sigh and a bowed head, he took her hand and followed, but not without first being given a final biscuit by Lady Catherine.

The conversation amongst the adults was not dull. It was as would be expected from family members reuniting after a time apart.

What cast a shadow on Mary's enjoyment was Richard. Not that he had done or said anything wrong. He had not. He had just been — she sighed to herself — perfect. He had entered into each conversation with vigor. He had teased his aunt on several occasions, and he had always given Alexander his full attention and spoken to him not as if he was a child of two but a young man capable of making wise choices.

The afternoon and evening had been as pleasant as they possibly could be when one was spending time with the desire of her heart, knowing full well that he would never be hers. There were moments when she forgot, of course, but then the remembering would happen and steal her pleasure.

"Are you well?" Elizabeth asked as Mary stood

at the bottom of the stairs. "You were very quiet at dinner."

"I am well. Just tired." It was not a lie. She did feel a minuscule amount of fatigue.

Elizabeth wrapped an arm around Mary's and looked up the stairs. "Shall we go up? Darcy and Richard must have their game of billiards before my husband retires, and Jane has already gone to bed." They began climbing the grand staircase.

Bingley and Jane had arrived shortly after tea. Jane had been tired at that time. One of her daughters was teething and had spent a great deal of their journey in a state of unhappiness. Therefore, both the child's parents were more fatigued than normal after a trip from town to Rosings and had retired early.

"I would like to pace the halls for a while if you are willing. I find a day in the carriage makes me restless." Elizabeth had always prized her walks at Longbourn and had not given up the habit after she married and moved to Pemberley.

Mary was happy to oblige her, for Mary had found the habit just as soothing as her sister. She only wished she had not waited until that first trip to Derbyshire to discover the activity. It would have helped her tolerate her mother and sisters so much better if she had taken solitary walks in Hertfordshire. That was the reason Elizabeth had taken them, after all.

"Do you like living here?" Elizabeth asked.

"It is pleasant," Mary replied. "Lady Catherine is not so difficult as I thought she might be. We get on quite well actually."

"I am glad." Elizabeth, after she had married Darcy, had come to understand Lady Catherine and her demanding ways. They were not meant to be imperious, though that is how they were often perceived. Her manners were just brusque and lacking in delicacy. Mary had never been given to great amounts of subtlety when provoked, so Elizabeth imagined there was a bit of a kindred spirit between the two. "I cannot believe Papa agreed to so long a stay."

Mary shrugged. "He thinks it is the best way to find me a husband. He knows Mama will not be promoting me before Kitty or Lydia. Not that I am complaining. I would rather not have Mama putting me forward."

Elizabeth laughed. "You have the right of it, in

my opinion. Sometimes it is best to not be her favourite."

Mary could not help but agree. To be pulled forward and thrust at a man while your accomplishments were listed was not something Mary wished to experience. They had reached one end of the corridor and began the trek to the other.

"You have not seen any gentlemen yet who catch your fancy, have you?" Elizabeth tried to keep her question light. She was curious to see if what Lady Catherine suspected was true.

"None that are within my sphere."

"Mr. Darcy was not in my sphere," reminded Elizabeth. "I would not discount a man simply for being of greater wealth than you."

Mary sighed. "Some men of a greater station are not wealthy. Nor am I."

Elizabeth's brow rose. It appeared that Lady Catherine was indeed correct. Mary had fallen in love with Richard. "That does make things more difficult," she admitted.

"Or impossible," muttered Mary.

Elizabeth leaned closer to her sister. "After coming to love my husband as I do, I do not believe in the impossible when love will have its way."

Mary's heart simultaneously hurt and rejoiced. She was happy that Elizabeth had found such happiness.

"Tell me," asked Elizabeth, "what has Lady Catherine had you doing to fill your time?"

"She has prescribed some reading, given me a sampler to stitch, commissioned a still life of roses, and taken me on calls nearly every day."

"So, life is full?"

Mary nodded. She did not want for things to do. "I am also required to practice my singing and playing on Mrs. Jenkinson's piano, which has been moved to my sitting room." It still seemed strange to have a sitting room of one's own. "I believe I will be fitted for clothes and a dancing instructor will be employed in June, if I have not found a husband by then." Every plan that was told to Mary by Lady Catherine was ended with that statement — if you have not found a husband by then. It was as if Lady Catherine knew of some mysterious gentleman that was going to appear and fall at Mary's feet.

"She is sparing no expense!" cried Elizabeth

"No, and I wish she would. I shall feel most wretched if I do not succeed in making a match."

"She mentioned a Mr. Breckinridge at dinner. She says he is about to take orders and expected to secure a living somewhere around here."

Mary sighed. "Yes, if I am not married by August, she expects to invite him to Rosings. As I understand it, he comes from a good family and is a third son. There is little chance he would ever inherit, but his family has connections and the living to which he is destined is not without merit. It is neither immense nor small but of a very respectable size."

Elizabeth laughed. "She is very well informed about him."

Mary lowered her voice. "She is very well informed on most newsworthy things and many that are not worthy of note as well. Has she told you about Mr. Emerson?"

Elizabeth shook her head. "No, I have not heard about him."

"He is an heir of a small estate in Surrey . He is not so handsome as some men, but he is pleasant and sensible and will be in want of a wife. The estate produces well, and as he is the sensible sort, there is little chance of a family going without. Mrs. Erickson, who lives just two miles past the church, is his aunt on his mother's side. She swears I would make him an excellent wife. Although she also said she did not think he could find another as pretty who would accept him."

"So he is a good deal less handsome than most men," Elizabeth said with a chuckle.

"That would appear to be the case," agreed Mary. "But, if I have not married by December, Lady Catherine will introduce me, for he is to visit his aunt at Christmas."

"Are you certain you would not rather have Mama promoting you?" Elizabeth teased.

Mary shook her head. "Lady Catherine assures me that she will not force anyone on me of whom I do not approve. Mama would not be so considerate."

"Indeed!" Elizabeth remembered well how her mother had tried to force her into accepting Mr. Collins's proposal. Thankfully, her father had been more supportive of her wishes. "Does Lady Catherine have any other gentlemen on her list?"

"None of whom I have been told, but I have only been here three weeks. There is still time to add to the list."

The sisters shared a laugh.

"Richard may be coming to stay with us for a time." Elizabeth cut a surreptitious look at Mary. "He is selling his commission."

Mary stopped walking. "He is?"

Elizabeth nodded. "I am uncertain of his plans in doing so, but I expect he will come for an extended stay with us until he has everything settled."

"Does he not have a house in town?" Mary asked.

"He does, but the country is so much nicer in the summer."

Mary had to agree. The air in the country was much fresher. "And he will not stay at Matlock?"

"He will likely divide his time between the two, and, if Lady Catherine has her way, he will be here for a time as well." Elizabeth smiled. "As much as she scowls and growls at his antics, I believe he is her favourite."

"She does speak of him often," said Mary. Far too often for Mary's sense of peace. She could not hear of him without her mind wandering down roads that led to marriage and children, and seeing as that was not something that would ever be, hearing of him was very disquieting. Richard staying here would not do, but then perhaps it would not be until after she was married. After she was married — she nearly chuckled at how Lady Catherine's comment was slowly integrating itself into her own thinking.

"He is enjoyable company," she admitted aloud. Too enjoyable, and therein lay the problem.

"I agree," said Elizabeth. "Some lady will be lucky to catch him, although he has not yet met with success in finding what he is looking for this season." The way Mary's eyes closed at the thought and the brief, painful expression that crossed her face was confirmation enough for Elizabeth. Mary loved Richard, and no matter how much Darcy might protest Lady Catherine's plan, she would not. She would speak to Lady Catherine tomorrow and offer whatever assistance she could to ensure her sister's happiness.

~*~*~

Richard placed his cue on the table. Darcy had beaten him once, and Richard was not in the mood to be beaten a second time.

"You are not yourself this evening," said Darcy, handing his cousin a drink before taking a seat in a large wingback chair. "Did the ride from town fatigue you or was it playing in the garden?"

Richard rolled his eyes. There were moments that his cousin was actually annoying and not in a follow-the-letter-of-the-law fashion but in a teasing way. This was one of those times.

"Neither," he replied, taking the seat across from Darcy.

"Then what has you out of sorts?"

And now, apparently, his cousin was going to slip from annoying tease into the equally annoying concerned friend and likely attempt to play the part of wise counsellor. Richard sighed. He was definitely out of sorts if he was thinking of Darcy in such terms. "Life, money, women, politics."

He shrugged as if it were not a matter of great importance that his life seemed to be held together loosely and would soon unravel into an unpleasant mess.

"Not the weather?"

Richard raised a brow at the return of annoying, teasing Darcy. "Not at the moment, but that might change."

Darcy shook his head. Richard was rarely so disagreeable. Not that the man did not become blustery about things, but to be curt and fidgety was not Richard's way. It meant, of course, that Richard was concealing something.

"Does all of this have to do with you selling your commission?" Darcy tipped his head and watched Richard's eyes grow wide at the question. "Aunt Catherine mentioned it."

"Indeed? I swear I have not said any more to her than to you on the matter." He scowled. "My mother, on the other hand, may have said a thing or two, which she might have heard from my father."

"Aunt Catherine is under the impression that it is a fait accompli."

Richard's head nodded slowly. "I believe it is. As you know, I have been considering it for some time, and with the war ended, now seems the best time."

"The militia will still be needed. It is not as if there is little unrest."

Richard again nodded his agreement. "There is plenty of unrest, but there is also an abundance of men who have served on the continent and who are now without a position. Many who are worse off than I."

"And you wish to serve your country in a different way." Darcy was not unaware of Richard's desire to enter politics.

"I do, but I cannot. Not yet."

"You need land."

"Land and money. Obtaining a seat is not without costs." Indeed, plenty of votes and, therefore, seats were purchased. It was not a thing of which he approved, but it was the way things were.

"With your father's backing, I should think you will find a place in the House without too much trouble."

Richard shrugged. "Perhaps, but I still need land."

"So we are back to marrying an heiress."

Richard drained the liquid from his tumbler. How he was beginning to hate that word and the fact that he was reliant on it. "Yes."

"There is no other way to get land?"

"None that I know of." Richard rose to refill his glass.

"Unless someone gives it to you."

Richard turned toward Darcy and shook his head. "No. I do not care how many acres you own, I will not be accepting any of it."

Darcy's brows furrowed. "Is there anyone from

whom you would accept such a gift?" Darcy knew that there was one person who seemed determined to help Richard in such a fashion, and he worried that it would be a struggle to get Richard to take the assistance. Not that Lady Catherine would set-tle for a negative reply.

Richard shrugged and shook his head. "No, I cannot think of anyone, save, perhaps my father. But he is not likely to divide up the estate, nor would I expect him to do so."

"Have you met any ladies that have interested you?"

The right corner of Richard's mouth tipped up. "None that will provide what I need." And therein lay the frustration. He knew exactly the lady he wished to take for a wife. A lady who was likely chatting with Darcy's wife at this moment. Unfor-tunately, that lady was not an heiress.

Darcy blew out a breath and scowled. "Politics are not worth such a cost!"

Richard watched the contents of his glass swirl up around the edge and fall back down. "I did not say I was denying my heart." He had not said it, but it was true.

"Did you not?" Darcy's tone was demanding.

"You, who trapped Elizabeth in my room so that I would have the desire of my heart, are willing to refuse my offer of assistance so that you might have the same."

"I did not say I have lost my heart," Richard snapped.

"Yes, you did." Darcy rose and walked to the billiard's table. It would be best to contradict Richard from a safer distance. "No one, but a lady one cannot have, makes a man as out of sorts as you have been this evening. Do you not remember my state of unrest on our last visit before I married Elizabeth?"

Richard did remember. Darcy had been sullen, deeply sullen, far more than normal. And short tempered! He had snapped and scowled and avoided Richard. Likely it was because Richard had been flirting with Elizabeth in an attempt to judge Darcy's feelings for the lady.

"Very well." Richard rose and drained the liquid from his glass. "I have lost my heart." He slammed his glass on the table next to Darcy. He very much disliked being forced to admit such a thing, and he also disliked having to think about just how lost his heart was to him and how unlikely it was ever to be restored. "Now you know. Are you happy?"

Darcy held Richard's glare. "I would be if you would allow me to assist you."

"That will never happen." Richard turned and left the room.

Darcy sighed. "That must happen," he said to the empty room.

Chapter 3

Mary slipped her feet under her blankets and leaned back against her pillows. Thoughts of Richard would not leave her be this evening. What she needed was a good serious read. She smoothed her blankets around her legs and took up the book from the bedside table. "Cowper?" Had she not returned this book to the library earlier?

She sighed. Obviously, in the commotion of people arriving and sweet nephews and nieces to distract her, she had left her book of sermons in the sitting room. "Well, I cannot leave it to morning, and, Mr. Cowper, you will not provide what I need, so, off we go."

She shoved her feet into her slippers and fastened her dressing gown snuggly about her waist. Then, with candle and book in hand, she made her way from her room to the sitting room to retrieve her book of sermons before stopping at the library to get rid of that tempting book of poems. It would not do to even have it in her room. Her mind was far too likely to talk her into reading one of the verses and dreaming about things she should not. No, it was best if she only had a book of reproving sermons to keep her mind from wandering down delicious trails.

She placed her candle on a table and closed the door softly.

"Miss Mary?"

Mary spun toward the voice. This was twice in one day that she had been startled by her name on his lips. And it was twice in one day that she had been holding that silent book of sermons having not yet read a word of them while being faced with the living breathing temptation of Richard Fitzwilliam.

"Colonel," she scooted across the room to the shelf that the book of verse called home. "I was just returning a book. Please do not let me disturb you." She glanced at where he sat at the desk writing a letter. He had obviously not expected company, for he was wearing neither coat nor cravat, his shirt was not tucked in, and his feet were only clad in stockings. It was such a lovely prospect seeing him so casually attired that her eyes demanded a second look.

"I shan't be long," he said, attempting not to lift his eyes from his letter. "I remembered something I needed to do before I retired and knew I would not sleep with it hanging undone over my head." He would likely not sleep anyway, but he was not about to admit that to the person who would occupy the thoughts keeping him awake.

She smiled at him when he looked up at her. "I fear, I am similar. I do not like to leave things undone." She moved toward the door. "Have a pleasant night, Colonel." She needed to escape to her room to read before she embarrassed herself by doing something silly like walking over to his desk to see what he was writing, or, more accurately, to smell the scent of him and to feel his presence next to her. She gave herself a mental shake. Such thoughts would not do.

She said one more farewell and attempted to open the door. It would not budge. She tried again. Still, she met no success. She tried a third time, this time using both hands.

"Colonel, do you have the key?" she asked,

turning toward him and attempting not to look or sound concerned even if her heart was anxiously racing.

"No, I do not." He gave her a puzzled look.

"The door is stuck," she explained. "I thought maybe if you had the key we could make the handle turn."

It felt as if a heavy weight had been dropped directly on Richard's abdomen. Darcy could not be doing what he suspected. "Is it locked?" he asked, though he was certain he already knew the answer.

She nodded, some of her anxiety showing on her face. "I think it is. I do not know how." She turned to look at the door. "I only closed it. I did not lock it. I swear."

Richard shook his head and sighed. "It is not you who has locked it." He remembered how, only an hour ago, Darcy had been discussing how Richard had trapped him and Elizabeth in a room to force them to come to an understanding. He shook his head again. "It was likely Darcy."

Mary turned toward him, her brows furrowed. "Why should he do that?"

"Turnabout is fair play, is my guess," muttered Richard.

"Pardon me?"

"Do you remember how your sister became engaged to Darcy?"

Mary's eyes grew wide, and she once again pulled at the door. "No, he would not."

Richard rose and crossed the room to jiggle the door handle. "It seems as if he has."

"Why?" Mary's eyes looked from the locked door to Richard and back to the door. He could not mean for her to marry Richard, could he?

Richard was not certain how his cousin had come to the conclusion that Mary was the lady who had stolen his heart, but it appeared Darcy's offer of assistance was not going to go unaccepted. "He must think we would suit."

Mary was beginning to feel a bit lightheaded and rather unwell. "But we do not." She wandered to the couch and sat down, feeling somewhat dazed. "Do we? You need an heiress, do you not?"

Richard took a moment to study the way she was pulling her feet up under her gown and curling into the corner of the sofa. He had seen her do it many times at Pemberley. There was a chair near a window in the library where she liked to curl up with a book, and as she read, her finger would wind and unwind a lock of hair that hung near the back of her neck. The sight had always entranced him. Even now, as she curled so small, he could not help feeling some of that bewitchment. "That is what I told him."

She nodded. "I am not an heiress." She blew out a great breath. "You will be ruined." She shook her head. "I should have stayed in bed and read those blasted poems."

Richard crossed to a window. He opened it and looked out. He didn't know why he was looking. They could climb out to the garden, but then where would they go? It was unlikely that anyone would let them into the house. The servants had likely been told not to open the door to either of them. It was equally unlikely that they would find any open windows through which they could re-enter the house. All this he explained to her when she asked if he thought they might escape.

"But, one of us might escape," she protested. "If the door is opened in the morning, and we are not found together, you will not be ruined."

"It is not the ruin of my aspirations that have me

42

concerned," he said softly as he took a seat on the sofa next to her. It was probably a bad idea to sit so close to her, but he could not resist. "And it is raining. Neither of us is dressed for rain."

"So we are trapped?"

He nodded. "It appears we are."

"You do not have to marry me," she said. "I could take a place as a companion or shift between Jane's and Elizabeth's homes to help care for their children. It would not be ideal, but it would not be horrid." She did not wish to be forced into a marriage with a man who would likely come to resent her for being the reason he had not been able to pursue the path he wanted to pursue. She could not bear to be looked at with disdain and regret by him. It would likely break her heart into more pieces than giving him up would.

"Is the prospect of being tied to me so horrible?" He had never considered that she would not like him. She had always been friendly and obliging and had seemed to welcome his presence. But perhaps she only thought of him as she did Darcy — as a brother.

"No, marrying you would be delightful." Her eyes grew wide, and she snapped her mouth shut.

"Delightful?" He smiled roguishly.

She swallowed. That smile was causing all sorts of curiously pleasant flutters in her belly. "Obviously, you are not a gentleman without charms," she explained as her eyes of their own volition strayed from where she had wished them to remain — on his face — to the breadth of his shoulders. "However, marrying me would not be good for your career. You need an heiress, and I am not one."

"I could ask Darcy for assistance. My aspirations may still be met."

She shook her head. "You would hate to be indebted to another man in such a way."

He chuckled. "It seems you know me well."

He was not wrong. She did know him well. Although the circumstances were not ideal, sitting here talking to him was lovely. She had always enjoyed the times they spent together talking, and she had listened to him carefully.

He pulled the book she held out of her hands. "Sermons?" He winked at her. "They still do not allow women to take orders."

She giggled. "A terrible oversight that."

He laughed. "I know you have mentioned wishing to marry a parson, but you have never told me why." He gave her a crooked grin. "I am not a parson, you know. Your aspirations will be completely shattered when you marry me."

"If I marry you," she corrected.

"When," he replied. "We are locked in a room. I will do the right thing by you."

"Only if I accept," she retorted.

He huffed. He knew that at times, Mary was as unyielding as his Aunt Catherine. She would likely refuse him if he did offer. "You know why I wish to enter politics, so it is only fair that I know why you wish to marry a parson."

She tilted her head and looked at him. He was handsome in broad daylight, but in the soft glow of the two candles in the room, he was downright enticing. "For many of the same reasons you wish to serve in parliament. I wish to help those who are less fortunate."

His left brow rose high in interest.

"Consider to whom people go when they are in need." She shifted to face him more fully. "The church. And who will be able to best help the women of a parish? The parson's wife."

"Could you not do more good if you were to marry a man of wealth?" he asked.

She shrugged. "Men of wealth are often tightly bound to their wealth, but I will grant you that being the wife of a generous landowner might give me more opportunity. However, there are inherent divides that arise between the needy and the wealthy. A woman in need might not be as willing to seek out the mistress of the estate as she would the parson's wife."

What she said made sense. There were class divides and sometimes those divides not only kept people apart but also created tension and strife. He had witnessed the plight and anger of the labourer who saw a landowner or manufacturer as the source of his destitution. He had even seen some of them hanged for having acted on that anger. It was these memories that moved him to attempt to bring change to the way things were through acts of government. She, on the other hand, wished to bring comfort and assistance through small acts of one woman to another.

"We are much alike, are we not?" he asked with a smile. They would suit well and do much good if they were to work together, whether in the realms of government or some lesser, more direct way. Perhaps he did not require a seat in parliament. And if he did not require a seat, then he did not require an heiress.

"It seems we are." She rubbed her arms. She was beginning to feel a chill from the dampness of the weather. Spring rains were not always warm.

"Come here." He motioned with his head for her to move closer to his side. "I can spare some heat to keep you warm. I mustn't have my wife become ill before she can refuse to marry me." He knew it was not a wise choice, but he could not allow her to shiver either.

She paused only for a moment to consider the danger of doing what he asked before she scooted over and snuggled herself into his side. They were locked in a room. It was likely they would be forced to wed. A small indiscretion such as this was of little significance, she reasoned.

But, oh, he smelled good. And he felt warm and solid. "I could read you a sermon to pass the time," she offered, hoping he would accept, and her mind would have something on which to focus besides the tingling sensation that his body pressed to hers created. She told herself she could move away to put distance between herself and temptation, but her heart and limbs would not listen.

He laughed and put the book on a table next to the sofa. "I would prefer poetry." There was a note of teasing in his voice.

"Poetry is inadvisable at present."

"Because you dislike those blasted poems?" His tone was still teasing.

"No" His hand running up and down her arm was making thinking a trifle challenging.

"Then why do you wish to read sermons over poetry?" He pressed her close into his side. Sitting here like this in the candlelight was so very unwise. And yet, he could not bring himself to act wisely.

"Poetry leads my mind to think improper things." Her answer was so soft that he had to bend his head towards her to hear it.

"About what?"

She bit her lip. She did not wish to tell him, and she determined not to tell him, but when he leaned toward her again and softly repeated his question, while his hand slipped from her arm to her hip, her determination crumbled. "About you," she whispered.

He was certain his heart had skipped a beat at

her admission and then restarted at a far higher rhythm. "Sweetheart," he murmured in her ear, "I do not need poetry to make my mind think improper things about you. A touch, a look, the sound of your name — it takes very little, and all I can think of is this." He knew he should not, but, just as his body had ignored every other warning about the lack of wisdom of his actions, it ignored this one as well, and he bent and kissed her. Softly. Just a taste. That was all he thought he wanted until he had tasted. Then, as she did not slap him or pull back or push him away. He delved deeper.

"We should not," she murmured as her hands threaded their way through his hair.

"I know," he answered as she pulled him back for another kiss. "But I want you."

"And I you," she replied. Oh, she knew she should not think such a thing, let alone admit it, but her mind constantly refused to comply with propriety when it was thinking about Colonel Fitzwilliam.

He kissed her again, pressing her backward. "I love you," he whispered as he nibbled her ear. "Darcy knows I love you. That is why he locked the door." He trailed kisses down her neck.

"Do you truly love me?"

He held her face in his hands and looked into her eyes. This woman, who lay beneath him, whose hands had slid from his hair to rest on his jaw as a finger traced his ear, was all he wanted. Not a seat in parliament and definitely not some lady of the ton even if she had bags of money. "Yes, very much. Marry me."

"But your future in politics," she protested weakly.

"The devil take politics. I have a home in town and am not without funds. They are not great, but there should be enough to do some good for those we meet. Marry me."

"You will not hate me for not being an heiress?" Her right hand slid from his jaw, down his neck, coming to rest on his firm chest right above his rapidly beating heart.

He smiled. "So long as you do not hate me for not being a parson. Marry me."

She nodded. "I will. I will marry you. Now, kiss me."

"If we continue, I am warning you that you may not be able to withdraw your acceptance." He kissed her forehead and then her nose.

Oh, she knew that she would not be able to refuse him a thing, not now, nor later. She paused for a moment as she attempted to think of some verse or quote from a sermon to help quell her desires. However, the only thing that came to mind — I am my beloved's, and he is mine — was of no use at all. They would marry, and all would be well. She ran a finger over his lower lip. "Kiss me," she said.

And he did.

Chapter 4

"Darcy, have you seen Richard?" Bingley asked as he entered the breakfast room the next morning. "He promised to go riding with me, and I have been to the stables and back twice already and have yet to see him."

Darcy shook his head. "The last I saw of him was last night before I retired." But Richard had been rather irritated when he had departed the billiards room. "Was his horse in the stable?"

Bingley nodded and paced to the window to look out in the direction of the stables. "He seemed out of sorts yesterday. Do you think he is ill?"

"Lovesick and stubborn, but otherwise sound."

Bingley swung around, wearing a wide grin. "Richard has found a lady?"

"He admitted as much last night — not that he did so willingly."

Bingley pulled out a chair across from Darcy and dropped into it.

"However, he believes he has no chance because she is not an heiress," continued Darcy, "and he refuses to allow me to help him."

Bingley leaned forward, an eager expression on his face. "But you will help him, will you not?"

Darcy shrugged. "He is stubborn." Likely not so stubborn as Lady Catherine, but getting Richard to accept assistance would probably be no easy task.

Bingley sighed and leaned back in his chair. "There must be some way. We cannot have him being the unfortunate one of our lot."

"There must be some way to do what?" asked Lady Catherine as she entered and took her customary place while a footman immediately brought her a cup of tea.

"Richard is in love," said Bingley.

Darcy shook his head and rolled his eyes. His friend had never been in the least bit intimidated by his aunt's presence. In fact, Bingley spoke to Lady Catherine as he would Jane or Darcy or any other friend, and Darcy expected it was something his aunt liked about Bingley. He was honest to a fault with her, withholding very little when asked.

"Yes, I know that," said Lady Catherine "But what are you scheming to do about it?" Her eyes fairly danced with merriment.

"Darcy offered him assistance, but he refused," Bingley picked up a roll and began to break it in half, earning him a raised brow from Lady Catherine, who picked up her knife and tapped his with it. Bingley placed the roll on his plate and sheepishly picked up his knife to complete the job of splitting the roll before he put jam on it.

"So you are scheming to find a way for him to accept Darcy's assistance?" She turned her amused look on Darcy. "I was under the belief that you did not wish to interfere with Richard and Mary."

"Mary?" Bingley's eyes grew wide, his knife hovered midway between the dish of jam and his roll. "Mary? As in our Mary? Mary Bennet?"

"Yes, our Mary," Lady Catherine replied. "Do not drip jam on my table, sir."

Bingley quickly brought the knife, laden with jam, to his plate, and Lady Catherine, after a muttering about speaking to Jane about her husband's manners, returned her attention to her nephew.

"Are you ready to help me with my plan, then?" She took a sip of her tea and then replaced the cup on its saucer before folding her hands in her lap and looking most satisfied.

"I believe I am." Darcy would do almost anything to ensure Richard's happiness. "I spoke to him last night, and he admitted to having lost his heart."

"But she is not an heiress," Lady Catherine's grin grew from a small smug one to a larger pleased-as-a-cat-with-a-mouse one. "And he needs an heiress to see his ambitions in Parliament to be realized."

Darcy nodded. "Yes, but he said he would not accept assistance from anyone." His tone held a warning.

Lady Catherine merely shrugged and continued to smile.

"Anyone," Darcy repeated.

Lady Catherine raised a brow. "You seem to think I would offer him assistance, but I will not."

Darcy's brows furrowed. "Did you not say you would see that he has what he needs to stand for a seat?"

"I most certainly did," she replied, returning to her cup of tea. "However, that does not mean I will be offering assistance because I know he is as proud as any man and will refuse."

Darcy's brows remained furrowed, and his mouth opened and shut as if he was at a loss as to what she meant.

Bingley nodded and smiled. "You shall trick him into it."

"I do not trick people," Lady Catherine said as she took a sip of tea and hid a smile behind her cup. "I arrange for them to make the best choice."

Darcy could not help but laugh at her comment. She had definitely been the one to set Richard on his path to trick Elizabeth into being locked in Darcy's room three years ago. Darcy would have said as much, too, but they were joined by his wife and Jane, and from the look on Elizabeth's face, all was not well.

She walked slowly to the table and took a seat next to him. "Have you seen Mary?" she asked softly. "She is not in her room."

Darcy's mouth dropped open again, and he turned to his aunt who was smiling and sipping her tea. "What have you done?"

She shrugged and placed her cup back on the table. "I have only ensured that my last remaining unwed nephew shall be happy." She took a key from her pocket and placed it on the table. "You will find both Richard and Mary in the library, where they have been all night."

"All night?" asked Elizabeth.

Lady Catherine nodded and rose from her seat. "You may wish to knock before entering — young lovers left to themselves and all that." She smirked and began to exit the room.

"Wait," said Darcy. "Why did you say you would give me until today to consider helping you and then lock them in the library before I could give you my response?"

She sighed. "Because as much as I love you, my dear nephew, you can be a touch too proper and slow to come to the point."

Bingley laughed.

"You did not expect me to help you?" Darcy folded his arms, looking rather displeased.

Lady Catherine shook her head. "No, I expected you to help me, but I feared you would attempt to remove some of the fun of the scheme. Plans such as these need to be executed swiftly and with clarity and with little emotion about how right or wrong it might be." She raised a brow at what she knew would be her nephew's retort. "The outcome is right, no matter the method employed."

Darcy shook his head. "I am not certain I can support such logic."

She smiled. "As I thought." She shook her head. "There was nothing wrong with what I did. If the two have not come to an agreement by the time you open the door, we shall make certain no word of this is ever spoken. My servants are faithful to me. Not one soul ever heard of you compromising Elizabeth from the mouths of one of my servants."

"I did not compromise Elizabeth. That was you and Richard."

"Was it?" his aunt asked with a grin. "I was almost certain that my parson said you were embracing his cousin."

Darcy rolled his eyes. Why had he even attempted to argue with her? She was well-versed at twisting and turning words to her advantage.

"Now, I will be in my sitting room when things of a serious nature such as contacting the lady's father and marriage articles need to be discussed." She looked pointedly at Darcy. "You will not leave me out of that discussion. It is imperative that you do not."

Darcy's brows furrowed. "Why? Richard is ... "

"I am not asking for Richard," she interrupted. "I have taken Miss Mary on and promised her father to see her well-matched. I will be there for her."

"But her father..."

"I will be there." Lady Catherine's tone brooked no argument.

"Very well," said Darcy. "You will be there if there is a need for such a meeting."

Lady Catherine winked. "Oh, there is a need," she said and chuckled as she left the room. She had peeked in the library window this morning when taking a stroll in the garden and had seen the way Mary and Richard were lying very cozily together on the sofa. There was definitely a need.

~*~*~

Richard squeezed Mary tighter and kissed the top of her head which lay just blow his chin. "Sweetheart, it is morning."

Mary stirred.

"They will likely open that door soon," Richard continued.

This comment made Mary's eyes pop open, and she began to disentangle herself from her sleeping position.

"Oof," Richard expelled a burst of air. "Careful, Sweetheart, your elbows are not so soft as the rest of you."

She scowled at him and shook her head. "I am moving as carefully as I can. I do not wish to just tumble onto the floor."

He helped her off of the sofa and laced his fingers behind his head as he watched her straighten her night rail and secure her dressing gown, a roguish grin on his face. "No, we would not want to tumble you on the floor. At least not right now."

Mary's cheeks flushed a brilliant red. "Please do not speak of it." She got down on her hands and knees and searched underneath the piece of furniture he was lying on for her slippers. "It should not have happened, and no one needs to know it did."

He propped up on an elbow and looked at her as she put on one and then the other slipper. Then he pushed to a sitting position and donned his shirt. He was feeling a bit chilled now that she was not lying on top of him to keep him warm. Her comments were also making him feel a bit uneasy. "We are to marry, are we not?"

Mary sat motionless on the rug, drew a deep breath, and expelled it. She knew there was no denying the fact that they must marry, but still her heart ached at being the cause of his not being able to achieve his ambitions.

"We are to marry, are we not?" he asked a second time, his heart beginning to beat just a bit faster and not in a pleasant way. When she turned toward him with her lip clenched between her teeth and concern in her eyes, he slid to the floor to sit next to her and pulled her to him.

"We are to marry," he said.

"I know we should after..." she paused, "our indiscretion, but..."

"No but," he said firmly. "We are marrying."

She nodded her head against his chest. "I wish to, and I know I must, but..." Her voice trailed off as she considered what marrying her would do to his chances for the career he desired. She tipped her head up. She could not see his eyes from this position, but she could see the way his jaw was clenched. "You will truly not hate me for not being an heiress? Not now, but in ten years when the children are running wild, and I am a fright?"

His jaw relaxed, and a smile spread across his face as he chuckled. "For one thing, our children will not be running wild. Neither of us would allow it — or at least, you would not. And I shall also be ten years older and quite possibly have a rounded gut and need a cushion for my gouty foot."

It was her turn to laugh at such an image. "You shall not be fat and gouty, for you do not sit still long enough for such to happen. You may be a bit softer perhaps, but not fat and gouty."

"And you shall not be a fright. In ten years, you will not even have a grey hair. I quite likely may, however." He arranged himself so that he could kiss her. "I promise you, Mary, I am attracted to more than your body," he waggled his brows, "as fine as it is."

She slapped her hand against his chest. "I asked you not to speak of it."

"Very well, but you will not be able to make me stop thinking about it." He kissed her again. "Now, how shall we arrange ourselves to be discovered?"

Mary looked at the window he had opened last night. "One of us could escape. The rain has stopped, and doors will be open."

"Are you trying to desert me before we have

even made our understanding known?" He said it teasingly, but secretly, he feared she might.

She shook her head. "No, I have given my word and will not renege."

He studied her face for a moment. "Are you certain?"

She was about to assure him that she was indeed certain when there was a rattling of a key in the lock, and she scrambled to her feet and flew to a chair near the window a great distance from him. It was bad enough that she had allowed her desires to overtake her good sense. It would be far worse to let anyone else know that she had done so.

Richard moved more slowly from the floor and sauntered over to the desk where his partially written letter still lay. He smiled at the words as he read them. Then, he folded the paper so that his words — the scribblings of a lovesick man — would not be seen by his cousin or whoever was about to enter the room.

Bingley nudged the door open and peeked his head around it. "Is it safe to enter?" he asked with a smirk.

"As you can see," said Richard gruffly.

"Do you still wish to go for a ride?" Bingley asked, giving a nod of greeting to Mary.

"Perhaps later," Richard replied. "At present, I would like to go to my room and make myself ready for the day, and then I would like some breakfast. And I am certain Miss Mary would like to do the same."

"Oh, of course," said Bingley, waving to the door. "I am to tell you, however, that Lady Catherine would like to see you as soon as possible." He glanced toward Mary. "Both of you."

Richard sighed. "We had expected as much, had we not, Sweetheart?"

Mary's eyes grew wide at the term of endearment, and she gave him a little shake of her head and a pleading look. "Yes, Colonel, I do believe we discussed that possibility." She rose from her chair with as much dignity as one who is found in a locked room with a partially dressed man and wearing her night clothes could.

Richard extended his hand to her. "Allow me to see you to your room, Miss Mary."

She breathed a sigh of relief that he had not addressed her as sweetheart again. As much as she enjoyed hearing him say it, it was not exactly the best way to be addressing her dressed as they were and in the predicament in which they found themselves. No one needed to know the particulars of what had transpired, at least not yet, maybe never, and such familiarity would give rise to too much suspicion. She thanked him and placed her hand on his arm.

He paused for a moment before escorting her from the room. "And where might I find my cousin this fine morning?" His tone was nonchalant, but Bingley looked very much as if he realized Richard was anything but blasé.

"I am not supposed to say," Bingley whispered, "but he is in your room, waiting for you." He looked apologetically at Mary. "And your sisters are in your room, I am afraid. They thought it best to discuss the ramifications of your predicament privately."

Richard shrugged. "I suppose ambushing us in our rooms is better than attacking us in here."

"Well," said Mary, looking sternly at Richard, "I, for one, am glad for the arrangement."

Richard's replying smile was full of mischief. "Then I shall be glad as well, Sweetheart."

Mary sighed and allowed him to lead her from the room.

Chapter 5

Mary stood in front of the door to her rooms.

"Do you wish for me to join you?" Richard whispered.

Mary could tell by the tone of his voice that he was not joking, and from the look in his eye, she was certain that he would indeed stand beside her as she faced her sisters if she asked him to do so. This little action spoke more loudly than any of the endearments he had whispered to her last night. She smiled and shook her head. "I will be well." Her head tipped to the side as she looked at him. "You will not harm Darcy, will you?"

Her eyes were again filled with concern, but he doubted it was actually for Darcy's welfare. He raised a questioning brow and waited, his silence begging her to continue. He needed to know her thoughts.

"You are not displeased..." Her brows drew together. "You do not regret..." She wished to ask whether or not he was entirely happy with the results of Darcy's scheming, but she could not find the right words to do so.

"I am happy to be tied to you." And he did appear to be happy.

Mary relaxed. All would be well. Would it not?

"However," he said, lifting her hand to his lips, "you frighten me each time you ask."

She blinked in surprise and opened her mouth to question him, but a maid scurried past, and she dared not.

"Go. Speak to your sisters," he said, kissing her hand once more. "We will finish this later." Reluctantly, he let go of her hand.

She turned and entered her room where her sisters were indeed waiting for her. Jane was seated at the piano, looking at a sheet of music, while Elizabeth was on the chaise reading a book.

"Are you well?" Elizabeth asked, looking up from her book.

Mary nodded.

"You cannot be." Elizabeth closed her book and placed it next to her on the chaise. "I was not well after being found with Darcy," she said. "And I was only locked in a room with him for two hours. You have spent a whole night with Richard. You cannot be well."

"I am," Mary insisted. She was not, but she also did not particularly wish to speak about it. She would rather have some time alone in her room to ponder all that had happened.

"Are you to marry?" Jane, who had crossed the room, placed an arm around Mary's shoulders and began to lead her from the sitting room to her dressing room.

"It seems we must."

Jane turned her and untied the robe that secured Mary's dressing gown. "Do you wish it?"

Mary drew a breath and opened her mouth, but then instead of speaking, she made a small whimpering noise and allowed her shoulders to droop.

Elizabeth and Jane shared a concerned look.

"Do you love him?" Elizabeth asked. "I got the impression when we were talking that you might."

"Oh, I do!" Mary cried. "So very much." Dressed only in her night rail, she sat down on the chair in front of the mirror. The sight of just how dishevelled her hair was caused her to blush.

Quickly, she took up the brush. "That is just the problem."

Jane opened Mary's wardrobe and removed a soft yellow dress. "How is loving him a problem?" she asked.

"I do not wish to be the cause of his disappointment."

"What disappointment?" asked Jane.

"He wishes to stand for parliament," replied Elizabeth. "However, he lacks funds and land." Her husband had told her about his discussion with Richard last night. "Darcy has offered him some assistance, but he refused it."

"As he should," said Mary.

"What do you mean 'as he should'?"

From the look on her sister's face, Mary knew Elizabeth was affronted by the comment. "A man has a certain amount of pride," she explained.

"I know very well about that," muttered Elizabeth.

Mary nodded. "Yes, your husband is a proud man, but not wrongly so."

Darcy always carried himself with a great deal of dignity, even when at Pemberley. The degree of his air of importance varied, of course, according to his situation, but he was never without the knowledge of who he was or what was expected of him in each circumstance. That was not to say he was not without error. He could at times, when he was displeased or uneasy, become rather disdainful. That perhaps was being wrongly proud, but Mary was wise enough not to point this out to her sister.

"Colonel Fitzwilliam is much the same, and to be indebted to another man is not an easy thing to accept and would necessarily cause him distress. It would be as if he were declaring a weakness to one and all."

"I do not think it a weakness to accept assistance," said Elizabeth as she poured water into the washbasin.

Mary shook her head. Perhaps a different approach was needed to help her sister understand Richard's hesitance in accepting Darcy's offer. "If you had not married, would you wish to spend your days reliant on the charity of your relations?"

Her hair was now not frightful, so she laid the brush back on the table and, rising, slipped behind a screen that stood between the washbasin and her sisters to see to cleaning herself quickly before changing into her dress and completing the task of fixing her hair.

"I would not enjoy it," admitted Elizabeth.

Mary knew it was likely as close as she was going to come to Elizabeth agreeing with her, and so she accepted the admission without further comment.

"Did you not speak of these things last night?" Jane asked. "Surely, you spoke of marriage and all that would entail."

"We did." She pulled on a fresh chemise and held her stays in place as Jane laced them.

"And what did he say?"

Mary blushed at the thought of how they had discussed his giving up his political aspirations. It was best not to repeat exactly what he had said, so she did not. "Despite his words, I am not certain he will not regret his decision."

"Is it not possible he could love you more than politics?" Jane worked on fastening Mary's dress as Elizabeth straightened Mary's skirt.

Mary made an uncertain harrumphing sort of sound. She had not considered that fact. She had just assumed a man gained his sense of worth from the position he held in society, not the one he held at home. She sat down at the dressing table and allowed her sisters to fix her hair.

As she watched them brush, twist, and pin her hair, she reviewed the times she had asked him if he would hate her for not being an heiress. Each time, he had looked....she tipped her head, and Jane tugged it back upright. He had looked fearful, and his tone this morning when asking her to reassure him that they would indeed marry had been anxious, and then he... Jane once again righted Mary's head from a tipped position. What had he said in the hall just now? That each time she asked, it frightened him? A smile touched her lips and peace tentatively crept into her heart. Yes, it might, just might, be possible that she was more dear to him than his ambitions.

~*~*~

"You are looking well," Darcy said as Richard entered his room. "A bit disheveled, but your mood does not appear to be as foul as it was last night."

Richard ignored his cousin completely and set about readying for the day. His man Stone had laid out all the shaving things he needed.

"Do you wish me to do it, Colonel?" Stone held a towel in his hand.

Richard nodded and, removing his shirt, took a seat, tipping his head back and closing his eyes.

"Are you tired, sir?"

There was a hint of impertinence in the younger man's tone, and Richard opened one eye and scowled at him.

"Do I smell lavender?" Stone asked.

Richard could hear Darcy chuckling. "Not unless you have put it in that soap you are smearing on me," Richard growled.

Stone set the soap and brush on the table and picked up the blade. For a moment, the only sound Richard heard was the scrape of the blade against stubble.

"I am certain I smell lavender, and there is none in the soap."

Richard opened an eye once again to peer at the man in displeasure. "You will smell only what I say you will smell, and you do not smell lavender." He, of course, smelled lavender as well. Mary had used some lavender cream when preparing for bed. It had made her skin smell as lovely as it felt.

"You cannot tell a man what he can and cannot smell," goaded Darcy.

"I believe I just did," Richard retorted. "And if he knows what is good for him, he will only smell what I say he smells."

"Right, Colonel," Stone agreed. "I shall ignore the smell of lavender."

Darcy chuckled while Richard growled. Richard wished Darcy would just get on with offering his assistance once again, for he was certain his cousin was going to do so. It was not as if Darcy needed to wait until Stone was gone. Richard was certain every man and maid in the house knew of his being locked in the library with Mary.

His eyes popped open, and he studied his man as he finished the work of shaving him. "Did you know of this scheme?" he asked. It had been Stone who had assisted him with the scheme to lock Darcy in his room with Elizabeth.

"What scheme would that be?" Stone asked cautiously.

"The one where I was locked in the library with a young lady for the night?"

"Of course," Stone replied as he wiped any remaining soap from Richard's face and neck. "We all had our instructions just like last time." He turned to put things away, but not quickly enough for Richard to miss the smirk he wore.

"And you did not inform me?"

"No, sir. I dared not."

Richard rose from the chair and began the rest of his morning ablutions. "You dared not?" he questioned.

"Forgive me for saying so," said Stone, " but your aunt can be terrifying when she chooses to be."

Darcy snorted.

Richard, half dressed and half clean and about to clean the remaining portion of himself, stopped. "My aunt?"

"Yes, sir. It was she who gave the instructions."

"Not Darcy?"

"No, sir. It was your aunt."

Richard looked at Darcy. "Was it not you who locked the door?"

Darcy shook his head. "Lady Catherine spoke to Elizabeth and me yesterday on our arrival about the possibility of needing a scheme to see you happily married, but neither Elizabeth or I agreed to assist her until today, which was obviously too late. You had already been trapped."

"Aunt Catherine locked us in?"

Darcy nodded and rising from his seat, paced to the window. "She says that no one need know of the situation if you and Mary have not come to an agreement. She assures me no one of the household will whisper a word." He turned toward Richard again. "Will there be a wedding?"

Not wishing to have this discussion while he was naked, Richard continued with what he was doing and then tugged on new trousers and donned a shirt before he answered. "I believe there will be."

Richard was not looking at his cousin, but he imagined Darcy's look of surprise that matched his tone when he asked, "You do not know?"

Richard sighed. "Mary seems hesitant."

"Have you offered then?"

Oh, he had offered — at least three times before she had accepted him last night. "Yes, I offered, and she accepted as long as I promised not to eventually hate her for not being an heiress." And he had promised more than once that he would love her despite that fact.

"I still stand ready to assist," said Darcy.

Richard nodded slowly. Perhaps he should consider accepting the help. Perhaps then, Mary would not feel insecure. He shook his head. She would likely feel guilty for having caused him to do something he did not wish to do. "I cannot accept it at present."

"What will you do?" Darcy asked.

Richard shrugged. "There are charities where I might be of use. It is not a grand country-altering method of seeing the lot of those in need improved, but it would be something. And I am not without contacts, I can petition those who have seats to make change."

"With your father's support thrown in, it might work," Darcy agreed. "However, if you do decide in the future that you cannot abide such a life, you need only ask."

Richard thanked him as he shoved his foot into his boot.

Darcy waited until Richard's man had quit the room before asking what he truly wished to know. "You do love her, do you not?"

Richard nodded, there was little point in denying it.

"And you are happy?"

"Happier than I ever thought I would be." It was the absolute truth. Although at one time, Richard had expected to be completely happy marrying an heiress of a compatible and pleasant nature for her wealth, he had, over the course of the past few months, realized that no matter how pleasant the lady, he would not truly be happy without Mary.

"Then why do I feel as if you are not as happy as you should be? Does she not love you?"

"Oh, she loves me, but therein lies the problem."

Darcy's brows furrowed. "How is that a problem?"

Richard blew out a breath. "It is a problem because I fear she loves me enough to refuse me so that I might pursue politics." He paced to the window and looked out. A seat in the House of Commons would be a great prize — an achievement of which he had always dreamt, but it would be hollow. He could work toward bettering the lives of the less fortunate, but what of his own life? A wife who would attend functions with him and then likely leave him to himself except for dutifully providing an heir was not the sort of mate for which he wished. He turned toward Darcy. "How did I ever think that a seat would be enough?"

Darcy grinned widely. "Duty often seems like it

is enough until we meet the women we cannot do without."

"Indeed," said Richard. He walked to his bureau and retrieved the letter he had been writing last night.

"Aunt Catherine will be waiting," cautioned Darcy as he saw Richard preparing to complete writing his message.

"Frankly, I do not care," he replied with a wicked grin. "You may tell her that since I had to wait a full night to be released from the library — where, by the by, there is a very grievous lack of biscuits — she can wait until I am ready to see her. Now, if you will give me a few moments, I have a task to complete."

Darcy shook his head. "She will not be pleased."

"Again, I do not care," said Richard.

"Very well, but please for the sake of the rest of us, including Mary, do not make us wait too long."

Richard held his pen suspended over the inkwell. "I would like to see Mary before we beard the lion."

Darcy shrugged as he opened the door. "Then you had best hurry."

Chapter 6

Richard refolded his letter and slipped it into his pocket. Then, with a last check of his jacket, he exited his room and, after pausing to listen at Mary's door, descended the stairs two at a time. How had she gotten ready so quickly? He had not dawdled at his task. He had been as quick as he could be. Ladies were not supposed to be quick at getting ready, were they? His mother never was.

Richard stood at an angle to the sitting room door and at a distance from which he hoped none would see him. There she was, seated on a settee, hands properly folded, back straight, and the smallest bit of the right corner of her bottom lip held between her teeth. As unpleasant as he imagined the upcoming meeting to be for himself, he assumed it would be worse for her. He had been scolded numerous times by his aunt — several of those times were purposefully caused. Mary, on the other hand, prized propriety, and, he doubted, was rarely the receiver of a reprimand, although he had heard her give many.

She turned her head just then, and he stepped into view. Her lips curled in pleasure to see him and her features relaxed. He drew and expelled a deep breath, and then strode into the room and took the seat next to her.

"It is so very kind of you to free your schedule to join us, Richard." Lady Catherine's voice dripped with sarcasm, and a slight smile graced her lips.

Richard looked at the tin of biscuits that sat on a table next to the settee. "I see Darcy delivered my message. It is not as good as a breakfast, but it will do until I can find one." He plucked up a morsel and popped it into his mouth.

"Tea has been ordered." Lady Catherine shook her head and chuckled. Richard had never been one to be intimidated by much. It was a quality that would do him well in the political arena.

"That is most appreciated," Richard replied with a grin.

"While we wait," Lady Catherine continued,

"we might as well get on with the necessary business."

Richard took another biscuit. "Do we have business to discuss?"

"I will thank you not to be impertinent," Lady Catherine snapped, and Richard nodded his acceptance. "It has come to my attention that a situation of a delicate nature has occurred."

"You mean," said Richard, "the one you created?"

Lady Catherine's eyes widened slightly.

"I am not angry," Richard assured. "However, I do not see a need to gallop around the pond to the left when the thing we need is on the right." He smiled at the confused look on his aunt's face. "I have not had my breakfast or a proper cup of tea, so the direct approach will clear the air much more quickly."

"Yes, I suppose that is true," Lady Catherine admitted.

"I have asked Miss Mary to marry me, and she has accepted." He rose to leave. "I think that concludes our business."

"Oh, for heaven's sake, Richard, take a seat,"

said Lady Catherine. "That is not the extent of our business."

"Is it not?" Richard said, returning to his place. He knew better than to push his aunt when she used that exasperated tone of voice.

"I will own that you are not pleased with me."

Richard shrugged but said nothing.

"It was devious of me to trick Miss Mary into going to the library with the intention of locking you in." She played with the hem of her sleeve and kept her eyes lowered. "However, it seemed the only way to see you happy."

"You tricked me?" Mary asked.

"You returned that book of poems to the shelf before you left for the parsonage," Lady Catherine gave her a small smile. "And I made certain that you forgot the book of sermons in the sitting room."

Mary's mouth dropped open.

Richard's brows furrowed. "How did you know I would be in the library?"

"I did not know you would be, but I suspected you might find it a welcome refuge after Darcy offered you his assistance." She paused and looked at Richard and then Darcy. "I knew he would. I had presented the idea of compromising you to him when he arrived and shared my concern that you would deny your heart." She shrugged. "You have often sought solace in a corner of the library. It is a quiet place to think — especially at night."

"You knew I hide there?" He had not thought anyone knew that about him. Most would retire to their rooms for solace, but he liked to be surrounded by the smell of books and the peace the room seemed to offer when the candles had all been doused, and everyone was in bed.

"Since you were a boy," she said with a smile. "Your father was the same. Whenever he needed to think deeply about some decision, he would do it in the library. Oh, he would work off his agitation on a ride, but when he needed to make a decision that weighed heavily on him, he would always steal away to a dark corner in the library." She tilted her head. "Had you come to a decision before Mary entered?"

He shook his head. "No." He had been on the verge of one, but he had not surrendered to it until later.

She looked at him for a moment longer. "About Darcy's offer..."

"No," Richard interrupted. "I do not need the assistance."

"You are still resigning your commission, are you not?" Lady Catherine asked.

Richard nodded.

"Good," she said, rising and going to the desk at the far end of the room near a window that looked out onto the garden. "Then you will be able to care for an estate."

"I do not have an estate," Richard said.

"Oh, perhaps not yet." Lady Catherine extracted some papers from her desk. "You will, of course, need to speak to Mr. Bennet, but I have written him of my approbation of the match. I will have it sent today." She sat back down and placed a letter on the small round table next to her chair. "He gave me leave to find a husband for his daughter, so I suspect, my approbation will assure you success, and then there will be no need to tell him of this little incident."

She smoothed the papers she held on her lap. "These should be taken to Mr. Bennet when you go." She held them out to Richard, who took them and leafed through them.

"I was left in a position to dispose of my husband's estate as I saw fit. Anne has no need or want of it, and I have no other children."

Darcy moved to look at the papers Richard held.

"I am also a woman without a voice in government." She smiled. "Until now."

Richard's mouth hung open as he read what was before him. She had given her estate, not to him, but to Mary. "How...?" He shook his head. These papers had been drawn up weeks ago.

"How did I know you would marry this lovely young woman?" She asked, smiling at Mary. "I saw it in your eyes, my boy. You adored her from your first meeting, and she was just as smitten with you." She chuckled. "It took a bit of scheming, but it has all worked out as it should."

Richard gave a small burst of incredulous laughter. "A bit of scheming?"

Darcy took the papers from Richard and read them again. "This is a lot of scheming," he agreed. He passed the papers to a bewildered Mary.

"It appears you are an heiress after all," said Richard as Mary began reading the pages.

Mary's eyes grew wide, and her mouth dropped open. She looked up at Lady Catherine unable to comprehend why this lady, who had known her only a short time, would give her something as large and valuable as Rosings.

Lady Catherine shrugged and dabbed at the corner of her eye. "This place needs a lady of determination and strength of character — as does my nephew. A weaker woman would see it fall into ruin. I also needed someone whom I could abide to see taking my place. There is a stipulation on one of those pages that says I will be allowed to live out my remaining days here," She lowered her eyes, "if you will have me."

"Oh, of course," Mary replied. Her mind was still trying to comprehend all that was happening. "It is your home." Mary handed the papers to Richard. "Are you certain you wish to do this?"

"I am. I have had a good life. My husband was loving and kind, and my child is happily settled. I wish the same for my nephew. A good life, filled with love. You will give him that."

Richard shook his head. "If you were giving Rosings to Mary, why did you lock us in the library?"

Lady Catherine shrugged. "I need you to chose her above all else, and you did, did you not when you were forced to do so?"

Richard nodded. "I did."

She reached forward and patted his knee. "A gentleman should always know his heart. However, sometimes a gentleman needs to be helped along the road to realizing where his heart truly lies." She pulled in a quick breath and released it. "Tea has arrived, and I believe you wished for a cup and some breakfast, did you not?" She pushed up from her chair and moved to the tea table.

Richard nodded as he flipped through the papers in his hands again. "Yes, tea would be lovely," he muttered. He shook his head in bewilderment and looked up at Mary. She looked happy, but if he was not mistaken, there seemed to be a slight hesitance to the smile with which she favoured him. "You will still marry me now that you are an heiress, will you not?"

She nodded.

"Are you well?" he asked softly.

"It is overwhelming," she replied. Her head felt a bit light if she were to be honest.

"Would you care for a bit of air? We could take a walk in the garden."

"I would, but tea would also be lovely."

"Then we shall have tea and then a walk." He lay the papers aside and, taking her hand, lifted it to his lips. "I love you," he mouthed. Then, having received a much better and a not-at-all-tentative smile, he turned his attention to his tea.

~*~*~

After a second cup of tea and a plate of breakfast, Richard finally found himself in the garden with Mary on his arm. He had intended to only have one cup of tea, but when his stomach rumbled, Mary would not hear of his going for a walk without having eaten. He pulled her close. How he had ever thought he could be happy without this woman right where she was at this moment was beyond him! They strolled contentedly and silently along the paths that marched at right angles to the flower beds and shrubbery. The order of the design with its straight lines and sharp turns pleased him.

"This will be ours," he said, breaking their silence. He turned and looked back at the house. "It does not seem possible."

"No, it does not," Mary agreed as they turned and once again began walking. "Are you happy?"

There was a small note of uncertainty in her question that made Richard's step falter. "I am," he replied. "Come. We will walk in the grove." He led her out of the garden and along the path toward the stand of trees. He wished for a few moments of her time without prying eyes watching him.

"I have something for you." They had stopped just a few steps into the grove, and he pulled his letter from his pocket. "It is what I was writing last night. I added a bit to it this morning."

"It is for me? You were writing to me?" She unfolded the letter.

"Those," he pointed to the top of the page, "are all the things I admire about you. They are foolishly sentimental and not well done," he said apologetically. "I am no poet, and I had not thought anyone would see them."

She could not help the silly smile that she knew she was wearing as she read of her eyes being described as pools of compassion and her hair as tempting tendrils. He had also written of her love of reading and the way she knew so naturally how to care for Alexander. There were a few other words that, though they were flattering, caused her to blush.

"As I said, I had not thought anyone would see that," he whispered, knowing of what she read by the pink tinge to her cheeks.

"You wrote these things before I arrived in the library?"

"Yes."

"Why?"

He pulled her a fair distance off the path and spread his jacket on the ground under a tree for her to sit on. "I had a plan," he said as he took a seat beside her. "I was going to write a short directive from a supposed friend asking me to return to London on urgent business. Then, I would ride out and send it to myself."

"Why?" she asked again.

"You were here."

She blinked. "Why should that matter?"

He sighed. "Have you ever wondered why my last stay at Pemberley when you were there was so short?"

"I did find it curious," she admitted. "And I missed you."

He brushed a wisp of hair off her forehead. "I could not keep my resolve to seek an heiress and pursue my course in politics when faced with all I have ever wished for in a lady, so I escaped. Or so I thought. But you would not leave me. I danced with numerous ladies and took them to the theatre and for rides, and I sat in many drawing rooms all the while comparing them to you. None of them touched my heart as you do. None of them stirred my desires as you do. None of them would speak to me as you do. They spoke of trivial matters, and not one of them ever glared at me for my impertinence." He smiled at the way she rolled her eyes. "They could have recited every sonnet of Shakespeare and explained the deepest tenants of philosophy, and still I would have found them wanting. And do you know why?" He brushed her cheek with the back of his fingers and then rested his hand at the nape of her neck. "They were not you."

He bent and kissed her startled lips gently and then rested his forehead against hers. "I could not find an acceptable heiress, nor could I write that letter to myself as intended because I could not bear the thought of being separated from you." He kissed her one more time. "I knew when I held you last night, even before I kissed you, that I would give my life to keep you there, at my side, shielded by my arms. Read the rest."

Mary did as he asked. They were but a few simple lines, written in the same scrawling hand and direct fashion as the words above had been.

My dearest Mary,

There is nothing — not wealth nor land nor politics, absolutely nothing — that I desire more than you.

Do not fear that I will stop loving you because I chose you over ambitions. I will not. You have saved me from a dire fate, for had I chosen ambitions over you, I know I would have grown to resent everything associated with that decision.

Love me, and allow me to love you. Give yourself to me again as you did last night. Be the mother of my children. Be the wife at my side. Be my confidant and friend. Marry me, Sweetheart, knowing that I do not offer for you out of duty but out of the deepest desire of my heart.

R.F.

The words were not eloquent, but they were dear. Mary read them a second time as tears slid silently down her cheeks. It was as Jane had said, and Mary had reasoned. He loved her more than politics. She lifted her tear stained, smiling face to him. "Thank you," she said as she threw her arms around his neck and hugged him tightly. "I love you so very much."

"You will no longer fear that I will grow to hate you?"

"No," she laughed and kissed him. "Never."

"And you will not think I am only truly happy because you are now an heiress?" One of his hands, which were holding her waist, slid lower and tugged her closer as he kissed her neck right below her ear.

She sighed at the pleasure of his mouth on her skin. "Not when I know you wrote those lovely things before I even knew I was an heiress."

He scooped his hands under her legs and lifted them as he pressed her backward with a kiss, gently lowering her to the ground. "If we were not so near the path," he whispered as he trailed kisses down her neck and across the top of her breasts.

She clutched at his hair. Oh, she was so very unable to deny him a thing. It was rather frustrating to find herself so wanting in propriety whenever he was near. It was not right, she knew, but...

"Then allow me to get up and kiss you in the thicket."

He captured her mouth for one more long, indulgent kiss and would have done as she asked had it not been for a very unpleasant interruption.

"I say, young man, this is not the place for such things!"

Richard groaned at the sound of hurried steps approaching them. He kissed Mary one more time before lifting his head and saying with a crooked smile. "Sweetheart, I think our parson has come to call."

Chapter 7

Mary's eyes grew wide, and her lips silently formed the word no before she scrambled to sit up.

Richard helped her right herself but would not let her stand as she wished to do. There were some things about being caught in a compromising situation that even he did not wish to put on display, so remaining seated seemed the best course of action.

"Mr. Collins," Richard nodded his head in greeting. "Lovely day for a stroll."

If his situation was not what it was and if Richard did not know just how mortified Mary must be, he would have laughed at the gaping, bulging-eyed expression on Mr. Collins's face. But he did know without looking at Mary that she was indeed uneasy. Her fingers digging into his arm where she held it was all the confirmation he needed. And to that end, he was trying to keep Mr. Collins's attention on him and not her. However, the man's eyes kept wandering back and forth between the two as his mouth flapped open and closed without producing words.

"Is Lady Catherine expecting you?" Richard asked. "Or is there an emergency at the parsonage?"

Mr. Collins blinked, his gaze becoming more focused. "No, no. No emergency," he managed to stammer.

"Mrs. Collins is well?" Mr. Collins was now looking only at Richard, and Richard intended to do his best to keep it that way by attempting normal conversation.

"Oh, she is very well," Collins replied.

"And the children? They are likewise well?"

Collins's head bobbed up and down in answer.

"So then you are on your way to visit my aunt as previously scheduled?"

Collins's eyes flicked over to Mary and then back to Richard. "No, it was not a scheduled call. Lady Catherine sent a message requesting that I call."

Richard nodded. His aunt was up to something. "Then you should not leave her waiting."

"But Cousin Mary..."

"Will be well," Richard completed the thought. "My aunt does not like to be kept waiting."

"But you and Cousin Mary were...."

"Passing the time," once again, Richard interrupted and did not allow the man to finish his thought. "It is a beautiful day for sitting outdoors."

"But you were not sitting,"

"We are now."

"But –"

"My aunt is waiting." Richard's tone demanded that the man in front of him stop speaking.

"But –" Collins attempted again.

"It is best for all if you do not keep Lady Catherine waiting." Richard rose from the ground and stepped closer to Collins. "Miss Mary will be well. I shall see that nothing dire befalls her. I will join you in the house if you wish, but I do not see a need to explain myself to you. And since Miss Mary is under my aunt's care and not yours, she also does not need to explain anything to you."

"Now see here. What I saw was most improper!"

Richard sighed. It was likely impossible to keep the man from sputtering a bit. "Oh, indeed, it was," he agreed, a half smile tipping his lips up on one side as the man before him was once again lost for words. Agreeing with accusations often had that effect on the accuser. "We will follow you in a few moments. It would be best to let Miss Mary straighten her clothes without your presence, do you not think?'

Collins nodded mutely.

"Good. Then, I suggest you continue on to the house, and we will follow." Richard grabbed the parson's arm as Collins turned to leave. "And it would also be most kind if you would not mention this indiscretion until we have arrived, and when you do, I would advise you do it with some dignity. I will not tolerate Miss Mary being humiliated by some ill-spoken word. You may say whatever you wish about me but not her. Do you understand me?"

Collins's eyes grew wide at the growling tone Richard used, and he readily nodded his head.

Richard released him, and once the man had scampered a fair distance down the path nearly to the entrance to the garden, he turned and extended a hand to Mary. "I apologize. I should not have allowed myself to be so overcome. It was badly done."

Mary straightened her dress and donned her bonnet. "I did not resist as I should have," she said with a small smile. It was not his fault that she had allowed him such liberties. She knew how to behave much better than her recent behaviour would indicate, but somehow when he touched her, all those sermons that she could recite to Lydia, flew from her head, and she became a wanton. She knew she should feel more guilty for her actions, but she could not. With Richard, it did not seem as improper as she knew it should.

He held his hand out to her again, and when she had placed her hand in his, he lifted it to his lips. "I should like to kiss you properly, but it is perhaps best if I do not."

Her brows furrowed and her lips turned down slightly. "I suppose you are right," she agreed sadly.

Chuckling, he pulled her into his embrace, gave her a quick kiss before releasing her and, with her hand on his arm, began walking back toward the garden and what he suspected would be a less than pleasant meeting.

He shook his head. Two such meetings in one

day! Perhaps it would be best if he rode to Long-bourn tomorrow and gained permission to marry Mary, and then, perhaps a special license could be acquired through his father more quickly than if he attempted it on his own. Haste was likely a good thing where marrying was concerned as it seemed both he and Mary lacked the self-control to behave appropriately. However, haste was not needed in returning to the house, and so it was twenty minutes before they reached the door to Rosings and another ten before they were in the sitting room.

Mr. Collins was perched on the edge of the green chair in which he sat. His hands were clasped tightly in his lap, and his right leg bounced nervously up and down.

Richard bit back a grin. It was apparent that his threatening tone had done its work in silencing the loquacious parson on the subject of what he had witnessed in the grove.

Richard greeted his aunt and Darcy before taking a seat in the same place he had sat earlier that day. As Mary took her place on the settee, he tugged her closer to him than was entirely proper and kept hold of her hand.

"Colonel," Mary hissed as she attempted to remove her hand from his.

"Yes, Sweetheart," he whispered back with a grin. Her eyes narrowed, and he reluctantly relinquished her hand. He sighed as she moved away slightly.

"It is about time you joined us, Richard. Mr. Collins has been eagerly awaiting your arrival to tell me something," began Lady Catherine. She was certain it was some bit of information about improper behaviour. It was partly her reason for summoning him when she did. She had hoped Richard would be a little improper. She had found it quite delightful over the last three years to fluster her parson on occasion. His responses were always so entertaining. Perhaps it was not right to goad him in such a fashion, but it was a refreshing change from his constant flattering. "I had thought he might expire of apoplexy had you been a moment longer."

Richard saw her lips twitch just the tiniest amount. His aunt was a scheming woman. He had always known it to be true, but until three years ago, he had never seen this slightly impish side of her. His father claimed it had always been there, but Richard had never seen it — until that meeting when she told him that it was time for Darcy to marry. "Do we not need to wait for the rest to join us?"

Mr. Collins's lips pressed into a firm line as if he were attempting to contain words from flowing forth unbidden.

"Bingley and Jane are walking, and Elizabeth wished to spend some time with Alexander," Darcy replied. "I am certain I can share whatever needs sharing later." His eyes twinkled with contained delight.

Elizabeth had had a softening effect on his cousin that Richard quite liked. Darcy was more willing to tease and taunt more like he did when they were younger and more carefree. He knew that Darcy would likely torment him later about what was going to be revealed, and that fact would not have bothered Richard had it not been for Mary. So instead of flashing his cousin a grin, he schooled his features into those of a serious gentleman.

"Any sharing will only be done if Mary allows it."

He held Darcy's gaze until he got a small nod

of agreement. Then, he allowed himself to wink covertly at his cousin. There was no need for Darcy to think he had overstepped some imaginary boundary by smirking when he had not. Darcy would understand the reason for Richard's seriousness was Mary. That was one very comforting thing about being so close to your cousin. Thoughts and feelings could be expressed nearly without words at times.

"Well, if we are quite ready," Lady Catherine said, "I have a project on which I wish to work while the sun is still bright."

Richard unbuttoned his coat. "I think it best if I ride to Longbourn tomorrow."

"I should say," muttered Collins.

"Tomorrow?" Lady Catherine's eyes grew wide, but Richard did not see any genuine surprise in them. However, he would play along.

"Yes," he replied with a small smile. "Mr. Collins caught me in a rather compromising situation, and so, instead of waiting to call on Mr. Bennet, it might be best to do it sooner rather than later."

Mr. Collins's brows drew together. "You intended to call on Mr. Bennet?"

Richard took Mary's hand and smiled at her. "We wish to marry."

"You do?" This was obviously not the way the parson had expected this conversation to go, for he seemed unable to contain his surprise in either his expression or features.

"We do," Mary replied.

"I asked Miss Mary for her consent last night, and we shared our joy with our family this morning," Richard continued, attempting not to look at his aunt's amused smile. He had learned over his years in the military how to deliver news in such a fashion as to make it sound acceptable, even if the circumstances necessitating the news were not pleasant. There was no need for Mr. Collins to know of last night's indiscretion, and so Richard only shared the basics of what had transpired.

"I do apologize for having been somewhat overcome with my good fortune," he bowed his head slightly as he looked at Mr. Collins, who blinked.

"Somewhat overcome?" repeated Mr. Collins incredulously. "You were –"

Richard cleared his throat.

Collins placed a finger on his lips for a moment

before continuing. "I am certain I can find it in my heart to forgive such an indiscretion."

"You are too kind," Richard replied.

Collins inclined his head in acceptance of the compliment. "It might be best to confine your walks to the garden," he suggested. "It is far less likely a thing for one to become overwhelmed with emotion when so close to the house where there would be proper chaperonage." He raised a questioning brow.

Richard nodded most seriously. "I shall bear that in mind." He looked at his aunt and flicked a brow up quickly. "Do you suppose it would also be acceptable to spend some time reading in the library?" he asked, pausing for a brief moment as Darcy coughed to cover a laugh before adding, "With the door open, of course."

Collins seemed oblivious to the fact that such a statement had been met with well-hidden merriment by Lady Catherine and Darcy.

"I should say it will depend on what is being read," the parson began.

"Poetry?" Richard gave Mary's hand a squeeze as he winked at her.

Mary shook her head slightly. Oh, he was tauntingly bad. He knew very well why she did not wish to read poetry in his presence or even when not in his presence.

Collins nodded thoughtfully. "Poems of nature might be best."

No, thought Mary, poems of nature were no better than love sonnets. Poetry, of any sort, made her mind wander down inappropriate paths. And now, having been so passionately kissed under a tree, her thoughts would likely roam even more than they had when she was unaware of the sensations a man could create in a lady.

"Yes, well, there are plenty of books to be read in the library," Lady Catherine interrupted before Mr. Collins could launch himself into some diatribe on the appropriateness or lack thereof of certain authors, books, and literary topics. She had heard many of his opinions on the subject and did not wish to hear them again, especially when she had things to arrange and news to pass along. "But that is not why I requested your presence."

Richard's brows rose at the slightly terse tone his aunt used. She must not have enjoyed the extra time he had deliberately given her with her parson.

"There is much to be done," she continued.

"There are guests arriving tomorrow. I must review the menu for Monday with my housekeeper and approve a plan for how the whole thing is to be laid out in the garden if the weather holds. And, then, I must also come up with an alternative plan if the weather turns foul, as it so often does in the spring." She turned to Darcy. "You do not think our guests will find it too cold to eat alfresco? It can be very impressive if done well, but I do not wish for any to become ill due to a chill."

A befuddled Darcy assured her that depending on the hour of the day, eating in the garden would be delightful and not at all uncomfortable. Easter was later this year, so the weather was therefore warmer.

"And then there is the sampler that I wished to finish, and Mr. Collins will wish to review his sermon for services tomorrow as well as Sunday." Lady Catherine stood and walked to a desk at the end of the room, the same one from which she had produced those surprising papers about Rosings earlier. As she walked and searched for another paper, she rattled on as if she was indeed concerned about all that needed doing. She was not, of course, since she had been planning for this event for more than a month now. "Having such a large portion of my family and his own in attendance will necessarily make Mr. Collins wish to prepare even more carefully than he already does. And he must review the wedding ceremony." She pulled a document from the drawer on the desk. "The earl will be here, Mr. Collins."

"My father?" Richard could not contain his surprise. "I did not know he was coming for Easter."

Lady Catherine's smile was a mingling of pleasure and secret. "Oh, he is not coming for Easter."

"He is not?" Richard's eyes narrowed and honed in on the paper his aunt was hiding behind her back. "Then, pray tell, why is my father coming to Rosings?"

"The same reason Mr. Bennet is coming," she replied with a look of feigned innocence. "The wedding."

Chapter 8

Lady Catherine had expected such an announcement to be met with exclamations, but it was not. It was instead greeted with wide eyes, gaping mouths, and silence. She considered explaining exactly what she had planned, but seeing as her audience seemed overwhelmed with what she had said so far, she thought it a wiser choice to follow their lead and keep her peace.

Mary was the first to find her voice. "What wedding?" she asked quietly.

Lady Catherine took her seat and smiled gently at the startled young lady. It was all well and good to perturb her nephew and her parson, but Mary... She sighed. She could not taunt Mary. Mary had never caused her the moments of consternation Richard had. "Yours, my dear," she replied gently, handing Mary the license she held.

Mary looked from the document in her hand to the lady across from her. It was the second time today that this woman had completely confounded her with a piece of paper. "I do not understand how you have this."

"My brother arranged it." Lady Catherine smoothed an imaginary wrinkle from her skirt. "After I obtained permission from your father for Richard to marry you, I wrote to my brother." She looked at Richard. "There is no need to call on Mr. Bennet. There never was."

Mary's eyes grew wide as she suddenly realized why Lady Catherine had spent so long in her father's study the day that she had come to collect Mary to take her to Rosings. "You planned this before I left Longbourn?"

Lady Catherine smiled sheepishly. "I began before that." She bit her lip and glanced quickly at Darcy. "It began at Pemberley on my last visit."

Mary's mouth gaped. "Is that why you spent so much time playing chess with my father?"

Lady Catherine nodded. "Although I do enjoy a good game of strategy." This drew a small burst of laughter from Richard, but thankfully, he did not insert himself into the conversation. She had to admire how he deferred to Mary when she knew he would like nothing better than to have his say.

"You were rather distraught when Richard left for London, and his departure was so abrupt — so very unlike him — that I knew my suspicions were likely correct. So, I laid them before your father and spoke to him in the most flattering ways about my nephew." She raised a brow at Richard. "I did not paint him with too rosy a brush, however. I felt it important for your father to know at least a bit about what a rapscallion he can be."

She took a deep breath and expelled it. "We parted knowing that Richard was not likely to follow his heart unless something in your circumstances changed, and so, after a long discussion with my daughter and my brother, I devised the plan to give you Rosings." She heard an enormous gasp from her parson and looked his direction to ensure he was not in dire distress before continuing. "However, as I told your father on my visit to Longbourn, I desired Richard to choose you before either of you knew of your good fortune. He was amenable as long as both you and Richard seemed happy with the results." Her eyes sparkled and her lips pursed as she held back a grin.

"My father knew you were going to lock me in the library with Colonel Fitzwilliam?"

There was another gasp from the man on Lady Catherine's left.

"Darcy, a glass of wine for Mr. Collins, if you will," she instructed before turning back to Mary. "He knew I planned to arrange a compromise much as I did for Darcy, but he did not know it would take place in the library."

"How did you know Colonel Fitzwilliam would choose me?"

"All men have their tells," Lady Catherine replied. "His is the way his eyes soften, and his lips curl into a small pleased smile whenever he sees you. That and I had heard tales about his reasons for dismissing several very eligible heiresses. It seemed to me he was only dismissing them because they were not you."

She turned here to Richard, who chuckled and shook his head in disbelief at the depth of his aunt's contrivance.

"I was correct, was I not?"

Richard nodded.

"But how did you know he...we would be happy with the results? If he were truly determined to follow his head and not his heart, he might have been only partially happy, and therefore, I would be equally as hurt by his inability to be completely delighted."

Lady Catherine shrugged. "I admit I was fearful of such an occurrence. The Fitzwilliam men can be foolishly stubborn. So, I had arranged that if the results were not as I expected, no word of this incident would ever be spoken." She smiled. "However, I knew before the door was open that my fears had been only the fluttering of a lady anxious to see those she cares about happy."

"How did you know before the door was open?" Richard's tone was leery.

Lady Catherine lowered her voice to a hushed but not altogether soft whisper. "The library has windows, and I have eyes."

"You saw...?" Richard could not bring himself to ask the full question.

"You were sleeping contentedly."

Richard breathed a sigh of relief that she was not going to say more. However, her next comment proved it might have been too early to relax.

"A quick wedding might be best, might it not?" she asked with a flutter of lashes.

"Indeed, it might," Richard agreed. "So when is this blessed event to take place?"

"Monday," said Lady Catherine. "It is best if the new master and mistress of Rosings marry in the church as is proper." She looked at her parson who was sipping on his wine and just beginning to look as if he might be ready to participate in any sort of discussion.

"Yes, my lady. That seems best," Mr. Collins managed to reply.

Lady Catherine smiled and thanked him. "Then, we shall have a feast for family and friends in the garden. Your mother, Richard, has seen to it that your house in town has been prepared to receive you for a short stay of say a week. Which shall give me time to install your things in your new master's apartment." She turned to Mary. "His is the room on the other side of your sitting room. I shall show it to you later today. I am certain you will approve of the decor, however. I took your preferences, such that I could gather from your sisters, into account, and I did do a credible job decorating your rooms did I not?"

"Do I not need to approve of the decor?" Richard asked. "I am to be the master, after all."

Lady Catherine shook her head and clucked her tongue. "And Miss Mary will be the mistress. Therefore, you will approve because your wife will be delighted. This is how it works."

Richard laughed and shook his head. "I am not certain you are entirely correct, but I will bow to your greater experience." He smirked at her scowl.

Lady Catherine rose. "I absolutely must see my housekeeper about the preparations, and there is a project that cannot be put off. A bride must have an appropriate dress for her wedding. It is too bad there will not be time enough for a trousseau to be ready before Monday, but it can be seen to when you are in town." She extended her hand to Mary. "I am certain the measurements your sisters gave me are correct, but we really must have you try the gown on in case it needs altering." She tucked Mary's hand in the crook of her elbow and leaned closer to her. "And I cannot wait to show you the detail I am adding." She sighed contentedly. "I should so like to be in town when Richard presents you at some soiree as his wife. So many disappointed ladies." She chuckled. "You will take her to at least one soiree," she called over her shoulder before exiting the room.

"She will likely come to town to ensure that I do," muttered Richard.

"Indeed," Darcy agreed with a chuckle.

Mr. Collins placed his empty glass on the table next to his chair and rose. "I shall go share the joyous news with my wife." He gave a small bow to Richard. "My congratulations to you on your good fortune, Colonel Fitzwilliam. May you both be very happy."

"Thank you. I believe we will be." Richard rose, walked with Mr. Collins to the door, received the gentleman's felicitations once more, and then returned to where Darcy still sat.

"Would you care to play a game of billiards?" Darcy offered. "Or would you prefer a ride?"

"Billiards," Richard replied. His mind was in a bit of a muddle with all that had happened so far today, and stalking the table and lining up shots seemed just the sort of thing he needed.

However, Mary did not find him in the billiards room later when her obligatory tour of the master's bedroom and wedding dress fitting were complete. No, Richard had not survived more than one game with Darcy. The taunting he knew he would receive was given in double doses as Bingley, who had just returned from his walk had joined them. Richard bore it as well as he could with several well-placed jibes of his own, but eventually, his need for time to think without any smirks or chuckles being had at his expense had won out over his need to stand his ground, and he had escaped to the garden.

Mary watched him as he sat on the ground rolling a ball to Alexander and then taking it from the child when he carried it back to his uncle. A tin of biscuits sat loosely covered next to Richard.

"She is beautiful, is she not?" he asked Alexander, who had trotted back to his spot and sat down. He nodded his head, and Alexander followed suit. "You are a bright boy."

He rolled the ball to his nephew, who immediately stood and, with ball in hand, walked to his uncle.

"But it is not her beauty that stole my heart," he said, taking the ball and lifting the lid to the biscuit tin for Alexander. "She is kind and intelligent and caring and determined, and so many good things. You will understand this one day. A wife should be more than a pretty face. Not that a pretty face is not also nice."

Alexander climbed onto his uncle's lap and looked up at him as if listening carefully while he ate his biscuit.

"And this garden will be ours — mine and Mary's, and I may be able to have a seat in parliament if I can get the right supporters. And you shall be able to visit me and your Aunt Mary in London as well as here and play with our babies."

"Mama?" Alexander asked, his brows furrowing into a serious expression.

"Yes, with your Mama and Papa." He ruffled the young boy's hair. "Will you like to have cousins?"

"He will likely enjoy them as long as they do not eat his biscuits," said Mary, coming to sit next to Richard. "I thought you would be with Darcy and Bingley, but you were not."

"I decided Alexander with his lack of vocabulary was a better discussion partner." Richard stood Alexander on his feet. "Get the ball," he said as he sent it slowly rolling.

Alexander giggled and trotted after it.

"Darcy was merciless in his teasing," Richard said in further explanation of why he was in the garden with a two-year-old rather than in the billiard's room with men of his own age. "Alexander thinks only of naps and bedtime stories when you speak of sleeping." He glanced at her with a crooked smile. "Gentlemen of Alexander's father's age think of more." Mary blushed as he knew she would.

She wrapped her arms around his arm that was closest to her and propped her chin on his shoulder as he took the ball from Alexander and rolled it again. "You are very good with him," she said. "You will be a good father."

He turned and kissed her cheek. "And you will be a good mother."

"Perhaps sooner than is entirely proper," she whispered.

"We marry on Monday. People do not judge the arrival of a child as improperly early if it arrives a few days before it should," he reassured her as he kissed her cheek again.

She sighed. "I do not know why I allow you to cause me to forget propriety, but I do."

"I do not find that to be a fault," he said with a roguish grin.

Alexander had returned for another biscuit and was beginning to rub his nose and eyes as he snuggled into his uncle's arms.

"I think it is time for this young man to return to the nursery." Richard shifted to rise.

Mary gathered the tin and handed the ball to Alexander to carry so that one of her arms would be free to link with Richard's, and so they proceeded to the house and up the stairs to the nursery.

Having deposited their charge with his nurse, Richard and Mary strolled the halls of Rosings, before settling on sitting for a while in the library. Richard insisted on pulling a book of poems from the shelf and reading one to Mary, who sat entirely too close to him to be completely proper and rested her head on his shoulder.

Mary sighed as he finished the poem and snapped the book closed. "I think I could come to enjoy poetry very much if you read it to me." She peeked up and smiled at him. "I love you," she said as he looked down at her. "And I am so very happy to be marrying you."

He slipped his arm around her and pulled her closer to his side just as he had done last night. "And I love you," he kissed her forehead, "and am also very happy to be marrying you." He shifted so that he could see her eyes. "And I know I would have eventually come to that point without my aunt's intervention." He kissed her gently and then repeated that he loved her.

Her eyes sparkled with delight and a touch of impertinence when he pulled away. "Even if I was not an heiress?"

He shook his head and chuckled. "Yes, even if you were not an heiress, for there are none who can compare to you."

"Kiss me," she whispered as her wayward hands found their way to his hair and pulled him closer. "Kiss me," she repeated when his lips were just above hers.

And he did.

Epilogue

Estella Katherine Fitzwilliam stamped her five-year-old foot and, with a huff, turned from the group of boys with whom she was playing and marched with fierce determination toward her mother.

Mary sighed and rose from where she was sitting having tea with her guests and moved to intercept her first born child. Estella had passion, heaps and heaps of passion. When she was happy, the world was blessed with her songs and praise, but when she was angry, it was a strong and foul wind that blew. And presently, the clouds looked as if they were gathering for a terrific storm.

"My daughter," Mary said, taking her child by the arm and steering her away from where Lady Catherine and the Collinses sat with Mr. and Mrs. Bennet. "You look displeased." It was an understatement, she knew, but it was always best when dealing with Estella to acknowledge that not all was right. The problem would then be aired with alacrity, and the damage of the howling winds could be diminished.

Estella huffed and crossed her arms as she looked back at the group of children. "He is a warty-faced toad!"

"Who is a toad?" Mary asked as calmly as she could. She knew the answer before it was spoken, but yet, she also knew that Estella needed to be the one to voice her opinions first before any sort of correction to actions or attitude could be made.

"Billy Collins." Her little foot stamped again. "He said I have lumpy mud on my head, and I do not. I have hair. And then Teddy said it was not mud but taffy, and Billy said that either way it was a frightful mess." Her lip quivered. "And Teddy laughed." A tear slid down her cheek and her father, who had joined his wife to lend his aid with their somewhat challenging daughter, scooped her up and held her close.

"I love taffy," Richard whispered into her ear. "Your hair is just like your mama's, sweet as a caramel wrapped in gauze."

Mary smiled at her husband's ability to calm their daughter. Estella had been born nearly nine months after Richard and Mary had married and just a few months after Theodore Darcy had been born. William Collins was only slightly older, having been born a month after Easter those five years ago. So, the children had spent many hours over the years playing together in Rosings' garden. And Teddy had shared even more time with his cousin when the Darcys and Fitzwilliams were in town or visiting at Pemberley.

"What were you doing right before Billy said you had mud on your head?" Mary asked as she rubbed Estella's back.

"Alex was telling us about a horse he saw, and we were trying to guess its colour." The answer was muffled against her father's jacket.

Richard winked at Mary. Their daughter was good at jumping quickly from one thing to another without always taking the time to consider the full situation before drawing a conclusion. That, he guessed, was likely what had occurred. Collins's boys might be a bit high in the step at times, but Darcy's were not. "Did Alexander say it was a beautiful horse?"

Estella nodded.

"And what colour was this horse?"

"The same as my hair, but Billy said it could not be since horses are not made of lumpy mud." Her tears had subsided, and her tone was no longer blustery but despondent. "And then Teddy said that my hair was the colour of taffy, and Billy said that horses are not made of taffy either, for horses of mud or taffy would not be beautiful but a fright-ful mess. And then Teddy laughed."

Mary sighed softly. That was the issue. Estella would have happily gone on her way playing with only a cross word or two for Billy had Teddy not laughed. Teddy was special to Estella. What he did was watched with fondness and what he said was oft repeated. There was very little that Teddy could do of which Estella did not approve. He was as dear to her as her sisters, Louisa and Grace.

"I would venture to guess that Teddy was not laughing at you, Sweetling," Richard said, placing Estella on the ground in front of him and crouch-ing down to look her in the eyes. "The idea of a horse made of mud or candy is a silly one, is it not?"

Estella's brows furrowed and her lips pursed in a pout, but she nodded.

"Can you forgive a boy for laughing at a silly thought?"

She sighed and slumped a little in defeat but assured her father that she could.

"Did you call Billy a toad?" Richard raised a brow and looked as stern as he was capable of doing when faced by one of his daughters.

Mary often teased him about how he had ever been feared as a colonel or won the respect of his fellow members of parliament if that was the best expression of displeasure he could conjure. Of course, she had seen him truly put out with one thing or another, usually due to some injustice he saw being dealt a less fortunate man, and she knew that he could be very gruff and justly harsh. She placed a hand on his shoulder and gave it a squeeze, glad that he was so gentle with their girls.

"Only to Mama." Estella looked at the ground as her lip trembled again. Displeasing her father, just like being treated unkindly by Teddy, was something that always brought a few tears.

"Good." Richard reached out and tipped her chin up so that he could see her eyes again. "You should not have said it at all, but at least, Billy did not have to be hurt like you were." He smiled at her as he said it and then wrapped her in his arms again. "Now, do you wish to return to Teddy or would you rather go find your sisters in the nursery?"

Estella glanced over to where Teddy was now playing a stick and ball game with Alex and Billy.

"I think a time of quietness might help heal the pain," said Mary with a smile, "and give your eyes and nose a time to become less red. Boys sometimes laugh at red noses."

Estella nodded and took her father's hand. "I will go to my sisters, Papa," she said.

"A wise choice." Richard winked at Mary. They worked well as a team. Not a one of their children had yet run wild, nor were they likely to if Mary could so capably maneuver a child with a wild bent, as Estella seemed to have, into doing what was best. "Shall we escort you?"

Estella shook her head. "I know the way."

"You will go directly there?" cautioned her mother.

Estella's head bobbed up and down.

"Very well. See that you do." Mary watched as Estella hopped and skipped toward the house, waving cheerily to Lady Catherine as she passed the group of adults, who were having tea.

"And you, Mrs. Fitzwilliam, do you wish to return to your parents?" Richard stood behind her and wrapped his arms tightly around her waist. Her figure had softened, but it was still one that he found irresistible. He peeked at the adults across the garden and then took a quick nibble on his wife's neck just below her ear.

Mary giggled and looked up at him. "You are very improper."

His brows flicked up quickly, and he gave her that roguish grin that always sent her heart racing. "As are you, my dear."

"Only for you," she assured him as she always did when he teased her about such things.

"I am not complaining," he replied as he released her from his embrace and offered her his arm. "Now, do we return to our proper place with Lady Catherine and your parents or do we go for a walk?"

"A walk," she said, placing her hand on his arm and allowing him to pull her closer than was entirely proper. "Grace is already a year."

"Yes, as of Saturday last." Richard wished to grin

at his wife's hidden suggestion and cart her off to a secluded spot, but instead, he chose to force her to suggest such a place, as he often did, much to her exasperation. "Do you wish to take a turn about the library? I could read that new book of poems that Lady Catherine so graciously gave you."

Lady Catherine had not ceased attempting to have some say in what Mary should or should not read. The fact that Mary often ignored her suggestions did not seem to fluster Lady Catherine in the least. In fact, Lady Catherine seemed pleased to be ignored, and then, would often wink at Richard and say, "A lady of substance with a spine to know what she likes is exactly what you need."

To which Richard would readily reply. "She is perfect, is she not?"

Mary would blush and roll her eyes, and Lady Catherine would merely chuckle and congratulate herself.

Theirs was a happy life, even when in residence at Rosings. Lady Catherine was a doting great-aunt and not at all as difficult to live with as Richard had at first feared. They got on quite well with only an occasional flare of tempers.

Richard credited Mary with that. She knew

exactly how to be firm with and yet understanding of Lady Catherine.

"Lizzy is reading in the library," said Mary, bringing Richard's thoughts back to the present. "I should like a place that is unoccupied."

They turned and started walking toward the edge of the garden. "The folly by the lake?" Richard suggested.

She shook her head. "No, too open."

"The grove then?"

She tipped her head and looked up at him with a small playful grin. "The thicket is well-grown over by this time, I should think." Her lips twitched as if she was about to laugh. "And our parson is already here, so..."

He chuckled and lifted her fingers to his lips for a kiss. "You know to what such impropriety might lead, do you not?"

"Indeed," she answered, "I hope it does."

Before You Go

If you enjoyed this book, be sure to let others know by leaving a review.

~*~*~

Do you want to know when the next Leenie B book will be available?
You can when you sign up to my mailing list.
Book News from Leenie Brown
(bit.ly/LeenieBBookNews)

~*~*~

Turn the page to read an excerpt of another one of Leenie's books

Unravelling Mr. Darcy Excerpt

The next book in the Dash of Darcy and Companions Collection is a fun, playful tale called Unravelling Mr. Darcy. The story begins, as you will see below, with Elizabeth giving Darcy a second chance immediately after his proposal — as in before he fled the parsonage. And Darcy is not about to fail in securing her heart this time!

CHAPTER 1

Fitzwilliam Darcy took one final lingering look at the lady who had stolen his heart, then crushed it beneath her dainty slippers. With some effort, he turned and willed himself to leave the parsonage even though his heart cried out for him to stay and plead his case. But what could he say? He had injured her sister in separating her from his friend.

The injury was not intentionally done, but it was done nonetheless. And *he* had done it.

She was also correct in that he had been aloof, but was that not to be expected from one of his position? He had to think of his family when choosing a wife. Did she not realize the great difficulty he would likely face in presenting a lady of little means, with a family seemingly devoid of manners that would recommend them, to the highest circles in the ton?

What she was not correct about was Wickham. But how could he defend himself on that account without placing his sister's reputation in jeopardy? Why could she not see that Mr. Wickham was too charming to be trusted? She was not unintelligent. She was actually very clever and, yet, also very duped by a charismatic deceiver.

His shoulders sagged under the weight of such tormenting thoughts as he pulled open the door to the sitting room and prepared to leave his heart behind, laying at her feet, with no hope of it ever being restored.

His steps faltered just a bit as he stepped out into the passageway. He closed his eyes and whispered a plea that he not be sent away from her. With a sigh of resignation, he placed his hat on his head. He had hoped there would be an instant answer to his petition, but perchance he was to be punished for having harmed another by suffering the same fate of being separated from the person he loved.

"Wait. Do not go."

Darcy turned slowly toward the door to the sitting room. Was his mind playing a trick on him? Was it making him hear words that he wished to hear but were not actually spoken? He had already learned that the orb between his ears was not to be trusted in its contemplations of Miss Elizabeth Bennet. It had been certain she would welcome his addresses. It had fancied her in love with him, and it had been wrong — horribly, cruelly wrong!

"Do not go," Elizabeth said once again when he turned her direction. "Please."

"Are you certain?" Darcy asked as he came to the door of the sitting room.

Elizabeth nodded. "I should not have spoken as I did." She wrapped an arm around her abdomen and took a tentative seat on a chair. "I was abominably rude and have no excuse to plead, save my indisposition." She rubbed a small circular pattern on her forehead between her brows as if to still the throbbing that lay behind her fingers.

Darcy took in the prospect of the woman before him. Her cousin had said that she had not come to Rosings due to a headache, and it looked to be a genuine malady and not just a ploy to avoid his aunt or for him to be able to find her alone.

He deposited his hat and gloves on a small table near the window that faced the front garden and crossed the room to sit near her. "You are unwell," he said, and then he grimaced. Of course, she already knew she was unwell. He did not need to tell her.

She smiled at him and opened her mouth as if to speak but then closed it again before rising quickly, one arm still wrapped tightly around her middle. "Please wait. I shall not be long," she said and hurried from the room.

For several minutes, Darcy paced the small sitting room, pausing each time he passed the door to listen for footsteps in the hall.

Quite obviously Miss Elizabeth was unwell and had remained at the parsonage because of that reason, and for that reason alone. He shook his head. Such arrogance to think she was possibly providing him an opportunity to make his offer! She had not been expecting his addresses at all. It was a sobering thought.

All of the ladies of his acquaintance who were not married, as well as a few who were, constantly put themselves in his path in an attempt to snare him for one reason or another. But not Miss Elizabeth. She didn't fawn over him or promote herself to him. She was different — in a most agreeable way.

She was intelligent and lively. He sighed. And beautiful — not in the fashion of the day. He shook his head again. No, in this way she was also different. Her features, to look at them with a critical eye, as he had attempted to do, were not classically beautiful, but her eyes — how they danced and sparkled, capturing her every emotion. Her smile lit her face. She moved with grace, and her figure was exceedingly pleasing — slight but womanly.

He stopped once more near the door to the sitting room to listen for her approach, and hearing footsteps, he hurried to stand near the mantle. It would not do to be found wringing his hands and hovering at the door like some anxious nursemaid.

He did a fine job of playing the part of an unaffected gentleman for a full ten ticks of the clock before he was propelled to her side by the ashen hue of her face.

"You are ill," he said as he assisted her to her chair. "May I call for someone to come sit with you? Is there anything that you require? I could send for the apothecary if you would like. In fact, I could fetch him for you myself." The words fell from his lips as rapidly as his grandmother's did when she was concerned and on the verge of a nervous fit. He clamped his lips closed and sat beside Elizabeth.

"I require nothing but a few moments of quiet," Elizabeth said, placing a hand on his knee, stopping it from bouncing. "The tapping of your foot," she explained when he looked at her in surprise.

He grimaced. It was not like him to be so very agitated, but then the lady sitting next to him had been unsettling him from the moment he had met her.

"I should go. You are in need of rest, and I am keeping you from it."

His voice was as apologetic as his look. If he stayed, he was likely to cause her greater distress than he had already caused.

"Are you certain there is nothing I can get you to ease your discomfort?"

He could use a good swift ride and a large burning drink. His every fiber seemed on edge.

She bit back a smile and that tauntingly impertinent eyebrow raised as she glanced at his hands which were rubbing back and forth on his knees. Immediately, he stilled them and rose.

"Please stay. I assure you my affliction is nothing out of the ordinary."

"But you are ill. Your head hurts, and I assume your stomach is unsettled," he protested as he began pacing. "You are in need of care."

"Mr. Darcy, please sit down."

Her tone was curt, and he immediately complied with a wary look.

"Your pacing was making me feel quite faint," she explained. "It is easier at the moment to look at you when you are still." She sighed.

His brows drew together, creating a worried crease as he looked at her. How could she wish for him to stay and claim that she was not ill? He could plainly see her discomfort. Her skin was not so ashen as it had been, but she was paler than normal, and her eyes did not contain the same liveliness. Would it not be better for her to go to bed and rest? He should insist upon that very thing, and he would insist if he were not so drawn to remain here with her. He had willed himself out of the room once already, and it seemed his heart was not in a state to cooperate a second time.

"I do not wish to be indelicate, sir. I assure you I do know what is right and proper," she began, her cheeks flushing to a more normal colour and then to a deeper hue. "However, since you have a sister who is in your care, I will assume you are not completely ignorant of the fact that at certain times a lady suffers from a particular indisposition. For some fortunate souls, it is a trifling matter. Unfortunately, I am not among the fortunate. So, as you can see, there is no need for concern."

Ah! He felt himself relax. This he both understood and knew how to assist.

"What you need," he said with a smile, "is a small glass of wine and a warming brick." He kept his tone soft and soothing. "Might I call for them?"

A small smile crept across her lips. "Your help would be most welcome."

He rose and, leaving the room, found the housekeeper and made his requests. Then, returning to the sitting room, he pulled a small footstool close to her chair for her use, took a small quilt that hung on the end of a chaise, and draped it over her legs.

"My sister, Georgiana, insists that warmth helps," he explained," unless it is summer; then warmth merely adds to her misery."

"You must be a good brother," Elizabeth said as she tucked the blanket around her waist.

"I wish I could say I am, but I fear I have failed her on more than one occasion." He walked to the door and stood looking down the passageway.

"Surely you are too hard on yourself."

"Do you think me incapable of failure?" His voice held a hint of anger. Her words accusing him of not being a gentleman still stung. He should likely not indulge that feeling at present, but the wound was too fresh to ignore. "I should think you would find me more than proficient in it."

She opened her mouth, and he expected a protest. However, no words fell from her lips before she closed them again. Her brows furrowed and her head tipped as she scrutinized him for a moment. Then with a bewildered look and a slight shake of her head, she again opened her mouth.

This time the action was accompanied by words, but they were still not a protest.

"I fear I accused you unjustly," she said.

Darcy lifted an eyebrow and folded his arms across his chest as he leaned against the door frame, waiting for her to continue.

Her head bowed. "I should have asked you about my concerns rather than racing to unfounded conclusions."

There was contrition in her tone, and he longed to ease her discomfort just as he did when Georgiana used such a tone. But, he would not. He held his peace and allowed her to continue.

"I am ashamed to say at times such as these, my temper often gets the best of my tongue and together the two can cause much damage."

He pushed off the door frame and moved into the room as a servant arrived with the wine and warming brick. "Place the brick on the small of your back, if you can, and sip the wine slowly. I would lower the lights to ease the pain in your head, but for propriety's sake, I dare not. However, if you feel the need to close your eyes, I will understand."

She shook her head but did as he suggested.

"You, sir, are an enigma," she said, situating the brick as he slipped a pillow behind her upper back. "I truly cannot make out your character. One moment you are lofty in manner, ordering and directing the lives of those around you, and the next, you are solicitous and gracious. You are a contradiction." She took a small sip of wine and then placed her glass on the table next to her chair.

Acknowledgements

As with all of my books, there are many who have had a part in the creation of this story. Some have read and commented on it. Some have proofread for grammatical errors and plot holes. Others have not even read the story (and a few, I know, will never read it), but their encouragement and belief in my ability, as well as their patience when I became cranky or when supper was late or the groceries ran low, was invaluable.

And so, I would like to thank Zoe, Rose, Betty, Kristine, Ben, and Kyle, as well as the lovely readers in my private Facebook group, Leenie's Sweeties, who read an advance copy of *Discovering Mr. Darcy* and sparked the idea for this story with their feedback.

I have not listed my dear husband in the above group because, to me, he deserves his own special thank you, for without his somewhat pushy insistence that I start sharing my writing, none of my writing goals and dreams would have been met.

Other Leenie B Books

You can find all of Leenie's books at this link
bit.ly/LeenieBBooks
where you can explore the collections below

~*~

Other Pens, Mansfield Park

~*~

Touches of Austen Collection

~*~

Other Pens, Pride and Prejudice

~*~

Dash of Darcy and Companions Collection

~*~

Marrying Elizabeth Series

~*~

Willow Hall Romances

~*~

The Choices Series

~*~

Darcy Family Holidays

~*~

Darcy and... An Austen-Inspired Collection

About the Author

Leenie Brown has always been a girl with an active imagination, which, while growing up, was both an asset, providing many hours of fun as she played out stories, and a liability, when her older sister and aunt would tell her frightening tales. At one time, they had her convinced Dracula lived in the trunk at the end of the bed she slept in when visiting her grandparents!

Although it has been years since she cowered in her bed in her grandparents' basement, she still has an imagination which occasionally runs away with her, and she feeds it now as she did then — by reading!

Her heroes, when growing up, were authors, and the worlds they painted with words were (and still are) her favourite playgrounds! Now, as an adult, she spends much of her time in the Regency world, playing with the characters from her favourite Jane Austen novels and those of her own creation.

When she is not traipsing down a trail in an attempt to keep up with her imagination, Leenie resides in the beautiful province of Nova Scotia with her two sons and her very own Mr. Brown (a wonderful mix of all the best of Darcy, Bingley, and Edmund with a healthy dose of the teasing Mr. Tilney and just a dash of the scolding Mr. Knightley).

Connect with Leenie Brown

E-mail:
LeenieBrownAuthor@gmail.com
Facebook:
www.facebook.com/LeenieBrownAuthor
Blog:
leeniebrown.com
Patreon:
https://www.patreon.com/LeenieBrown
Subscribe to Leenie's Mailing List:
Book News from Leenie Brown
(bit.ly/LeenieBBookNews)

Made in the USA
Monee, IL
12 November 2022